Mooch

AN ALDO ZELNICK COMIC NOVEL

Written by Karla Oceanak

Illustrated by Kendra Spanjer

BAILIWICK PRESS

Also by Karla Oceanak and
Kendra Spanjer — Artsy-Fartsy,
Bogus, Cahoots, Dumbstruck,
Egghead, Finicky, Glitch,
Hotdogger, Ignoramus, Jackpot,
Kerfuffle, Logjam, All Me, All
the Time, Goodnight Unicorn

Published by:
Bailiwick Press
309 East Mulberry Street
Fort Collins, Colorado 80524
(970) 672-4878
Fax: (970) 672-4731
www.bailiwickpress.com
www.aldozelnick.com

Manufactured by:
Bang Printing, Brainerd, Minnesota, USA
March 2018

Book design by:
Launie Parry
Red Letter Creative
www.red-letter-creative.com

ISBN 978-1-934649-76-3

Library of Congress Control Number: 2018931292

27 26 25 24 23 22 21 20 19 18   7 6 5 4 3 2 1

To my marvelous
munchkin*—
I will miss you,
but I hope your
wilderness adventure is
as memorable* as you are.
I'm mad about you*!
Goosy

Mr. Zelnick,
A modicum* of advice,
man to man—make sure
there is method to
your madness.*

Munificently,*
Mr. Milton Melville Mot

WHO'S WHO

MOSQUITOES
(EVERYWHERE)

HIM, MARVIN
SHOEMAKER

ME, ALDO
ZELNICK

MARVIN'S MOM,
ANIMAL LOVER

MY MOM,
THE FRESH AIR
AFICIONADO

MAX, BEST
DOG EVER

MY COMIC
CHARACTER,
BACON BOY

MOOCHY, MAGICAL MAGPIE

ABERT'S SQUIRREL

MULE DEER

MEXICAN SPOTTED OWL

ELKS

WILD TURKEY

MOUSE (A.K.A. SCARIEST BEAST EVER)

SKELETON

MOUNTAIN LION, AS IN, AN <u>ACTUAL LION</u> THAT LIVES IN THE MOUNTAINS

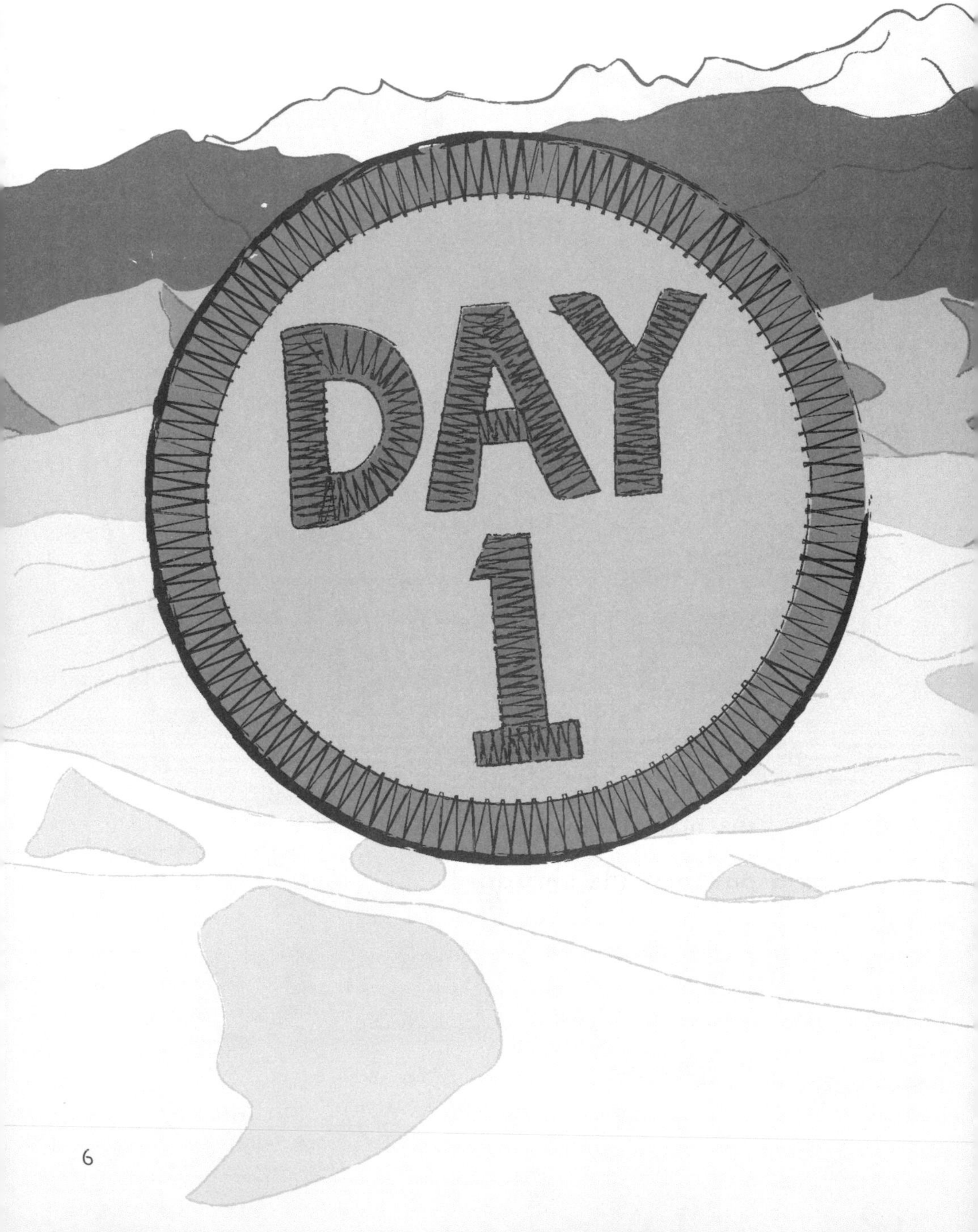
DAY
1

MIDWAY* TO MESA VERDE*

BLECHH!!!

I spit out the mouthful of water I'd just borrowed from Marvin's water bottle. "It's <u>warm!</u> And it tastes like wet feet!"

Marvin is a kid from school and now—thanks to this June hiking trip our moms devised—my camping partner. He shrugged.

"Water is water," he said.

We were standing atop a massive pile of sand. All around us, sandy mound after sandy mound.

7

Yep, turns out the tallest sand dunes in all of North America are in my state, Colorado, which last time I checked is nowhere near the ocean — or Aladdin-land. —

WHERE WE LIVE

MESA VERDE PARK

SAND DUNES

TO THE MIDDLE EAST*

"Now I've got the munchies,*" I said to Marvin, moving on. "What's on the snack menu?"

Marvin plopped his backpack onto the dark-pancake-colored sand. He unzipped it and said, "Granola bar. Trail mix. Beef jerky..."

I reached for the meat and tore open the package. I was just lifting the morsel* to my mouth when a flying monster landed on my arm, grabbed the jerky with its beak, and winged away. I might have screamed bloody murder,* just for a millisecond.*

"*Pica hudsonia!*" called a voice. It was my mom, yelling up to us from the base of the dune. "A black-billed magpie!"

I slid down to Mom and Max (our dog). "That bird," I explained, "basically <u>mauled</u>* me!"

"Don't be silly," she said. "Magpies are harmless, but they <u>will</u> steal your food if you're not careful."

"Magpies are mooches,* all right," said Marvin's mom, Mrs. Shoemaker. She's an animal doctor and my mom's friend. "Magpies are called 'camp robbers' for good reason."

Marvin sprinted down the sand hill, waving his notebook. His favorite speed is sprint, I've noticed. "Wait!" he said. "I need to write this down for my bird badge."

According to Marvin, he's an exceptional outdoorsperson. He's been in Cub Scouts since he was born, and he just graduated into Boy Scouts. I know this because this morning, on the million-mile car ride from where we live at the top of Colorado to this sand park at the bottom of Colorado, he kept showing me pages from his notebook.

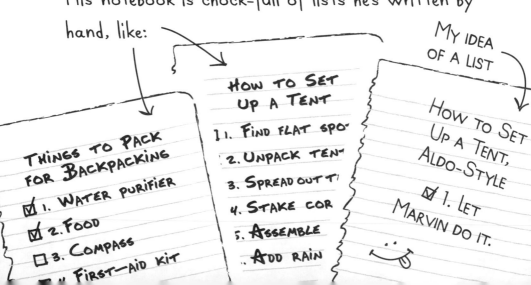

I'M MORE OF A SLEEP SCOUT.

Turns out Marvin's a very by-the-book guy. His notebook is chock-full of lists he's written by hand, like:

MY IDEA OF A LIST

THINGS TO PACK FOR BACKPACKING
☑ 1. WATER PURIFIER
☑ 2. FOOD
☐ 3. COMPASS
    4. FIRST-AID KIT

HOW TO SET UP A TENT
1. FIND FLAT SPO'
2. UNPACK TEN'
3. SPREAD OUT T'
4. STAKE COR
5. ASSEMBLE
.. ADD RAIN

HOW TO SET UP A TENT, ALDO-STYLE
☑ 1. LET MARVIN DO IT.

In case you don't know me yet, I am <u>not</u> an exceptional outdoorsperson. I do not like OUTSIDE. I do not like sweaty activities. Hiking is cruel and unusual punishment, uphill. Hiking for 5 days straight is...welp, I've been trying not to think about it.

OUR MOTLEY* HIKING CREW

"Let's talk more about magpies in the car," said Mom as she herded us all back into our minivan. "It's still 4 more hours to Mesa Verde, which is where we'll set up camp for tonight."

Just 4 more hours of air conditioning, I thought. *Sigh.*

Also in case you don't know, my mom is a bird fanatic. It's a big reason we're on this trip. She hopes to find and take pictures of a certain rare owl that lives only in a certain rare spot.

WHO.
WHO.
WHO, ME?

The other reason we're on this trip is middle school.* Blerg. A couple of weeks ago Mom told me I need to get more mature* over the summer, so I'll be ready for 6th grade. She thinks camping and hiking will make me manlier* or something. I told her I'm already mega-mature for my age and don't need to sleep on dirt to prove it.

"Plus, I have 2 beard hairs coming in," I said when she first mentioned the trip.

"So do I," Mom said. "And we're going camping."

"At least can Jack come instead of Marvin?" Jack's my best friend. Marvin's...eccentric.

"I've already made plans with Mrs. Shoemaker," she said. Conversation closed.

Fine. I got this. I can take care of myself. I'll show her—<u>and</u> Marvin the Magnificent.*

10 MATURE THINGS ABOUT ME

1. DOUBLE-DIGIT AGE (11)
2. ELEMENTARY SCHOOL GRADUATE
3. ANTIPERSPIRANT USER (ONCE)
4. SMARTPHONE (MOM'S OLD ONE)
5. CLEAN ROOM (UPON REPEATED REQUEST)
6. GOOD COOK (THANKS, DAD!)
7. STURDY BUILD
8. MUSCLES LURKING UNDER STURDY BUILD
9. RECENTLY SHAVED HEAD IN MANNER OF MARINE*
10. MELTDOWNS* IN PAST WEEK: <u>ZERO</u>

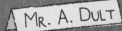

MR. A. DULT

MOREFIELD CAMPGROUND

I'm sketchbooking this by the light of our campfire. The moms and Marvin are already asleep, so it's just me and Max marveling* at the moon, which is almost as round as a paper plate.

When we first got to this campground at Mesa Verde National Park earlier today, we set up two tents—one for the moms, one for the menfolk.* Inside the tent, I rolled out my sleeping bag and garnished it with my big, fluffy pillow. Then we prepared our evening meal.

FOOD IS BORING. LET'S EXPLORE.

AHHH... A NICE MEDIUM-RARE* STEAK WITH GRILLED GARLIC MUSHROOMS FOLLOWED BY VIDEO GAMES AND A RELAXING CAMPFIRE. YES, LET'S EXPLORE THE COMFORTS OF THIS CAMPSITE.

After dinner, the moms and Max went for a walk, and Marvin ran around the campground doing this scavenger hunt where you have to find and check stuff off a list, like shrubs and signs about baskets and cave paintings. Me, I relaxed in my camp chair and played Minecraft on my laptop, thanks to the campground's wifi! Wuuut!

Pretty soon some mule deer* walked by. "'Sup, deer," I said and took a picture of them with my phone.

Next some wild turkeys walked by. "'Sup, turkeys," I said. Snap. Another epic pic.

Then a magpie landed on our picnic table. He sat there for a long time, fixing me with his jet-black eyeball. Could it be the same moochy bird who stole my meat morsel a hundred miles from here? I took a picture of him too.

I had to Marvin-sprint away from camp, though, when a mouse scurried by. Those things are scary!

Next, my mom made us hike to Point Lookout—uphill 1 mile!—just so we could see the views of Montezuma and Mancos Valleys below. Meh.* Still, I did not complain.

When we reached the mountaintop, Mom showed me and Marvin how to get found if we're ever lost in the wilderness. My eyes were too closed from tiredness to watch, but I heard a couple of things she said, like "jump up and down" and "look at yourself in a mirror." Yeah. They didn't make sense to me either. Plus, I have my phone. I can call people if I get lost!

After the hike it was getting dark, so we ambled over to the campground store, used the real bathrooms, bought ice cream bars, and headed to the amphitheater for the ranger program. We sat outside with a bunch of other campers on rows of wooden benches. Marvin balanced his notebook on his head.

A park ranger taught us about constellations, which are basically connect-the-dot star pictures in the sky. He said that on a clear night we can always tell which direction is which by finding the North Star. It's at the end of the Little Dipper's handle.

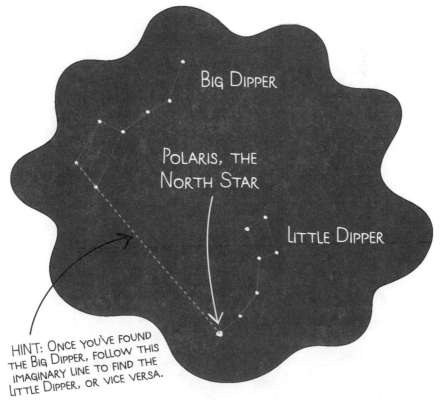

BIG DIPPER

POLARIS, THE NORTH STAR

LITTLE DIPPER

HINT: ONCE YOU'VE FOUND THE BIG DIPPER, FOLLOW THIS IMAGINARY LINE TO FIND THE LITTLE DIPPER, OR VICE VERSA.

Post-star-lesson, we returned to our campsite. Mom made me try starting the campfire without matches, by spinning the end of a stick against a scrap of wood. But that was <u>way</u> too tiring, so after a minute I snuck Mrs. Shoemaker's matches from her pack instead. Once the fire was roaring, we toasted marshmallows and made s'mores.

HOW TO MAKE A S'MORE:

GRAHAM CRACKER

TOASTED MARSHMALLOW

CHOCOLATE CANDY BAR SQUARE

GRAHAM CRACKER

Turns out I'm an outdoorsperson after all! I'm great at camp cooking. The wildlife adores me. And I'm a star master! Marvin might be an official Boy Scout, but I'm the one who's just naturally good at this stuff. I'm not sure my mom noticed yet, though. Or Marvin. Tomorrow I'll make sure they do.

ALSO, I'VE GOT MAD* S'MORES SKILLS.

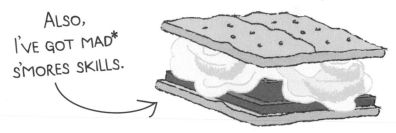

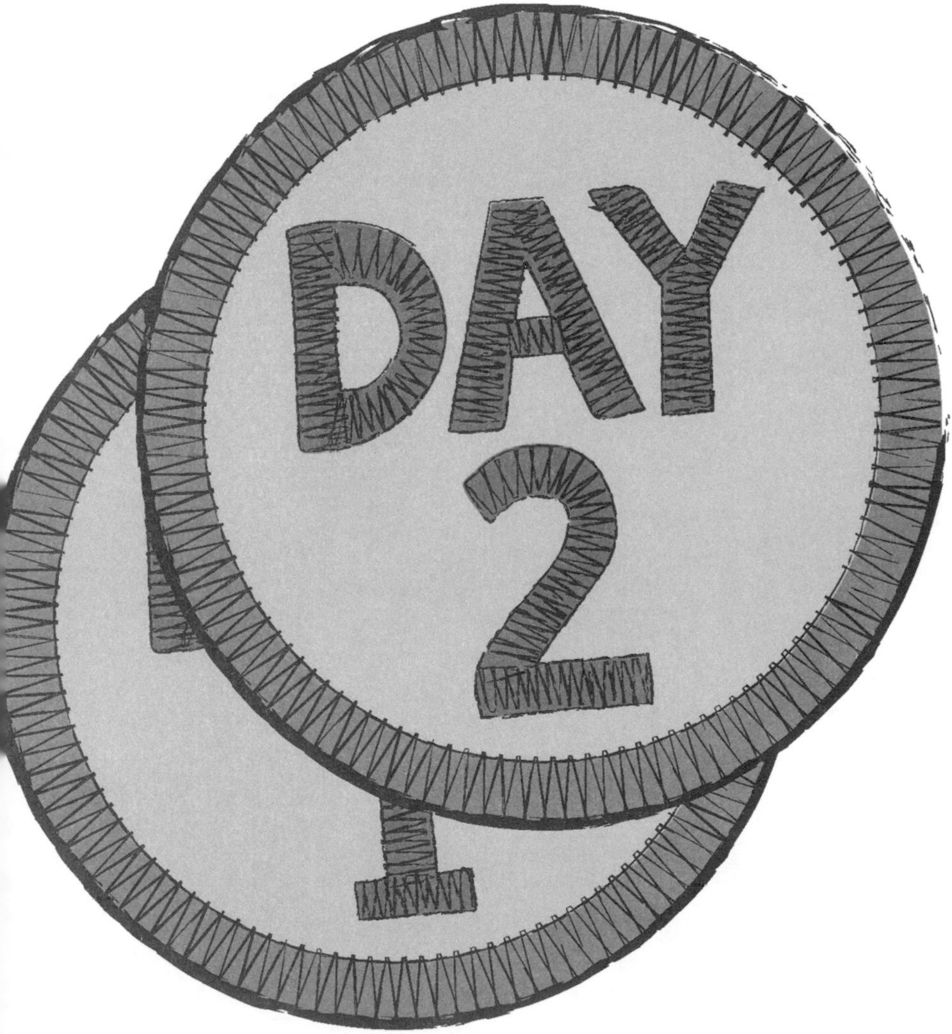
DAY
2

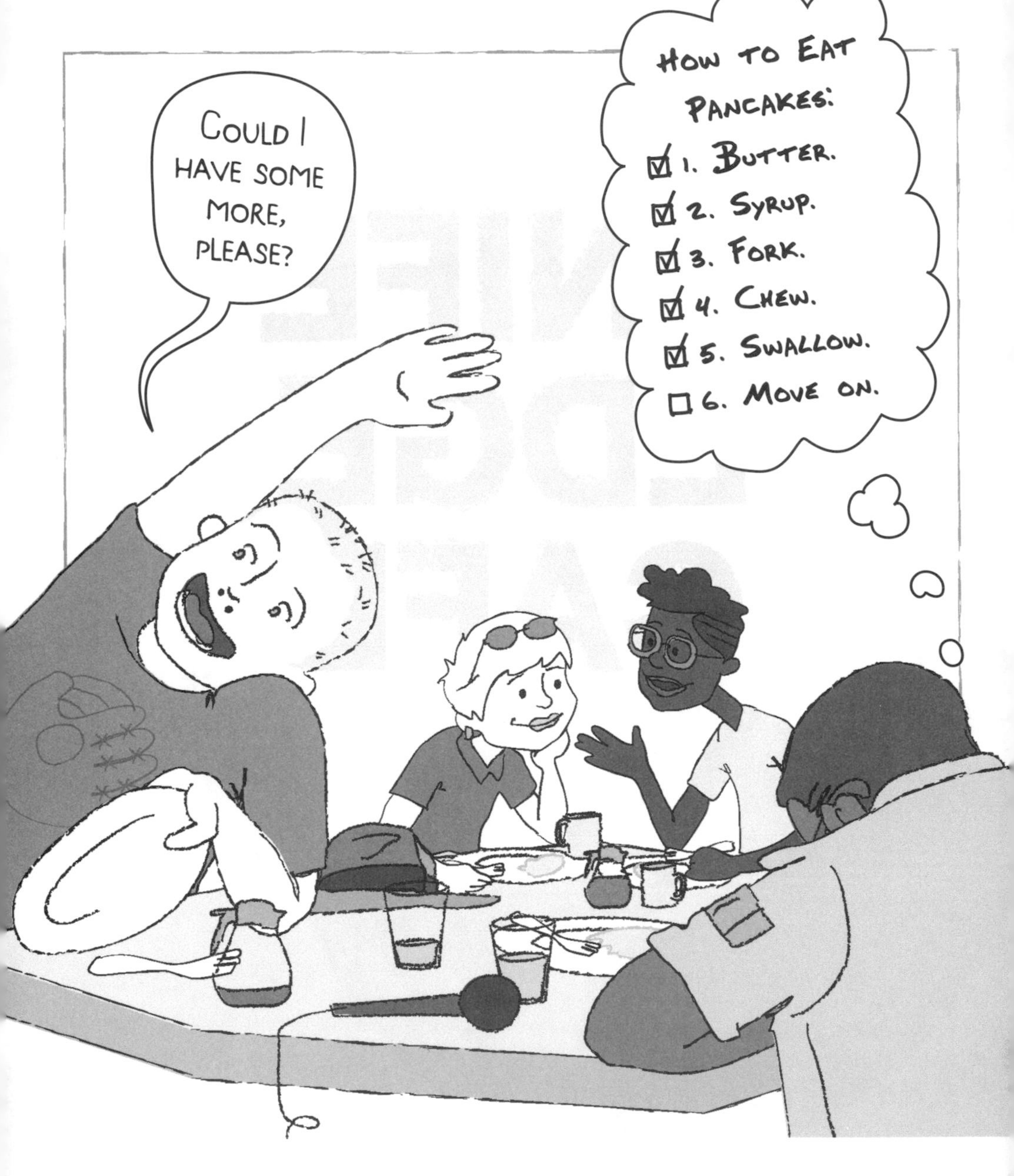
COULD I HAVE SOME MORE, PLEASE?
HOW TO EAT PANCAKES:
☑ 1. BUTTER.
☑ 2. SYRUP.
☑ 3. FORK.
☑ 4. CHEW.
☑ 5. SWALLOW.
☐ 6. MOVE ON.

MESA VERDE

Even though I'm not a morning person,* this morning started out quite nicely, with an all-you-can-eat pancake breakfast at the campground café. 9 flapjacks later and I was Prepared for the morning.

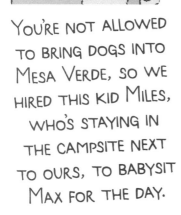

YOU'RE NOT ALLOWED TO BRING DOGS INTO MESA VERDE, SO WE HIRED THIS KID MILES, WHO'S STAYING IN THE CAMPSITE NEXT TO OURS, TO BABYSIT MAX FOR THE DAY.

Then we drove into the park on a long, twisty road, which was lined with dead stick trees. My mom explained that lightning sparks wildfires here all the time, and the fires annihilate everything that burns.

"Looks like a scary movie...," I muttered.*

"What's that, Aldo?" asked Mrs. Shoemaker.

"Er...I said it looks very groovy!" After all, mature outdoorspeople appreciate all the outdoors, even the burnt kind, right?

Marvin looked askance at me then returned to his notebook.

Inside the park, our first stop was Chapin Mesa Archeological Museum, where we watched a movie about the Ancestral Puebloans. They're the people who lived at Mesa Verde from 1,500 years ago to 800 years ago. Basically, they liked to grow corn, eat cactus fruits, and make baskets and pottery. (Actually, just the moms and I watched the movie. Marvin couldn't sit still. He ran around the museum making lists in his notebook instead.)

After the movie we wandered past displays of historical stuff, like ears of corn and pottery bowls. Behind glass panel after glass panel were little models of the Puebloans' stone-and-mud buildings and naked action-figure-sized people going about their ancient lives—cooking, basket-weaving, hunting deer with spears. Etcetera.

Yes, I said naked.

Well, mostly naked, anyway. Apparently the Puebloans weren't big clothing fans. Marvin pointed and chortled, but I remained cool as a cucumber, even though my own mother was standing beside me.

"Yes, the people of Mesa Verde were quite ingenious," I declared maturely as I headed for the exit. "Shall we proceed to the great outdoors?"

The 4 of us picnicked then walked down a hill, where we stopped to watch a park ranger demonstrate how to build a survival shelter. Marvin paid attention and even made a list in his notebook, but since we brought tents on this trip (hello!), I chose to hunt for special rocks to bring home to Jack instead. Rocks are his thing. A weird squirrel with lanky ears joined me.

PONDEROSA PINECONES ARE __MY__ THING.

"'Sup, squirrel," I said and took a picture of him. "I'd give you a real snack, but...I didn't pack any."

After the ranger program we continued on to Spruce Tree House. Which is not a treehouse at all. It's an old brickish fort on the side of a hill. Marvin and I stepped down a log ladder into the dark, chilly, mysterious basement.

"This room is called a kiva," whispered Marvin, reading from his Junior Ranger booklet. "It was like their church."

YA KNOW, SKETCHBOOKS ARE _MY_ THING.

WELL NOTEBOOKS AND LISTS ARE _MY_ THING.

On the ladder climb out of the kiva, I lost my grip on the fat logs and tumbled back down. Luckily, Marvin was right behind me to break my fall.

"Ouch, dude," I said, dusting myself off and giving him a hand up. "I guess we've learned an important outdoor safety lesson."

Marvin bent to pick up his glasses, then he shot past me and up the ladder. I mosied* out and met up with everyone. Mom said it was time to hike again.

I wanted to mutiny,* but that's not what a naturally good outdoorsperson would do.

So instead I mustered* a grin and headed down Petroglyph Point Trail. Marvin and his mom sprinted ahead, allowing my mother and me to go slowly and really appreciate all the physical activity. She took a million pictures of birds while I put 1 foot in front of the other.

I was just getting really hot and sweaty
when we came to a mural on a big rock wall.
We stopped to marvel.

"Whoa...," I said.

"I knew you'd like it," Mom said. "These are
petroglyphs—pictures engraved with rock tools."

"By aliens?" I asked. "Because that guy
there looks like an alien. And that weird handprint
definitely belongs to an alien!"

"No, not aliens," Mom said. "Puebloans. It
tells the story of two ancient groups of Puebloans
who were migrating to a new home."

"Pretty sure it's aliens. And look at that bird
drawing! It's a magpie!" I gasped. A shiver danced
down my backbone. Even as I spoke, I noticed that
my enthusiasm was making it hard for me to keep

calm and mature. I took a deep breath and sat to sketch the alien mural. "I'm rather thirsty," I said politely after I'd copied down the petroglyphs.

"Where's your water bottle?" Mom asked.

"In the car."

She glowered at me. "You can't survive without water, Aldo. You have to carry it at <u>all times</u> on this trip. OK?" She handed me hers.

"Water is heavy." I frowned then maturely swallowed both the water and my annoyance. "But, you're right, Mother. OK." Moms. Sheesh. They act like everything's a matter of life and death.*

Just then, guess what landed on the rock mural? A <u>real</u> magpie. Was the same magpie following me? It blared its irritating cheep then flew right past my newly crumpled hat.

I turned to my mom. She arched an eyebrow. "Looks like the magpie might be your spirit animal," she said.

"What does that mean?"

"Some Native Americans believe that each of us has a certain type of animal that protects and guides us. Maybe the magpie is yours. Maybe it's trying to tell you something."

"So it's like a mascot*?"

"Kind of."

I was dubious, but I didn't say so. If mascot animals were part of the mature outdoorsperson deal, then I'd go along with it.

"Hey, I'm getting pretty good at this hiking thing, aren't I?" I said after a bunch more dusty steps.

"I'm noticing some improvement," Mom said. "How are you getting along with Marvin? He could use a friend."

"He's a pain," I wanted to say, but I knew that wasn't the answer she was looking for. Instead I said, "I'm noticing some improvement."

By the time we made it back to our minivan, Marvin and Mrs. Shoemaker were finishing a <u>second</u> hiking trail.

"Take it easy," I whispered to Marvin. "You've gotta pace yourself."

"This is my pace," he said. "Your nose is red."

Oops. Sunscreen. Back at home, Mom had given me a tube to pack, but I forgot it. And this morning when she asked me if I'd put it on, I'd said yes. Because otherwise, lecture—and loss of all the matureness credit I've earned so far.

COOLEST MASCOTS

BECAUSE EVERYONE WOULD BE AFRAID OF YOU

BECAUSE YOU COULD FLY. PLUS AMERICANS WOULD LOVE YOU.

BECAUSE TOP OF THE FOOD CHAIN!

BECAUSE <u>MAMMOTH</u>*!

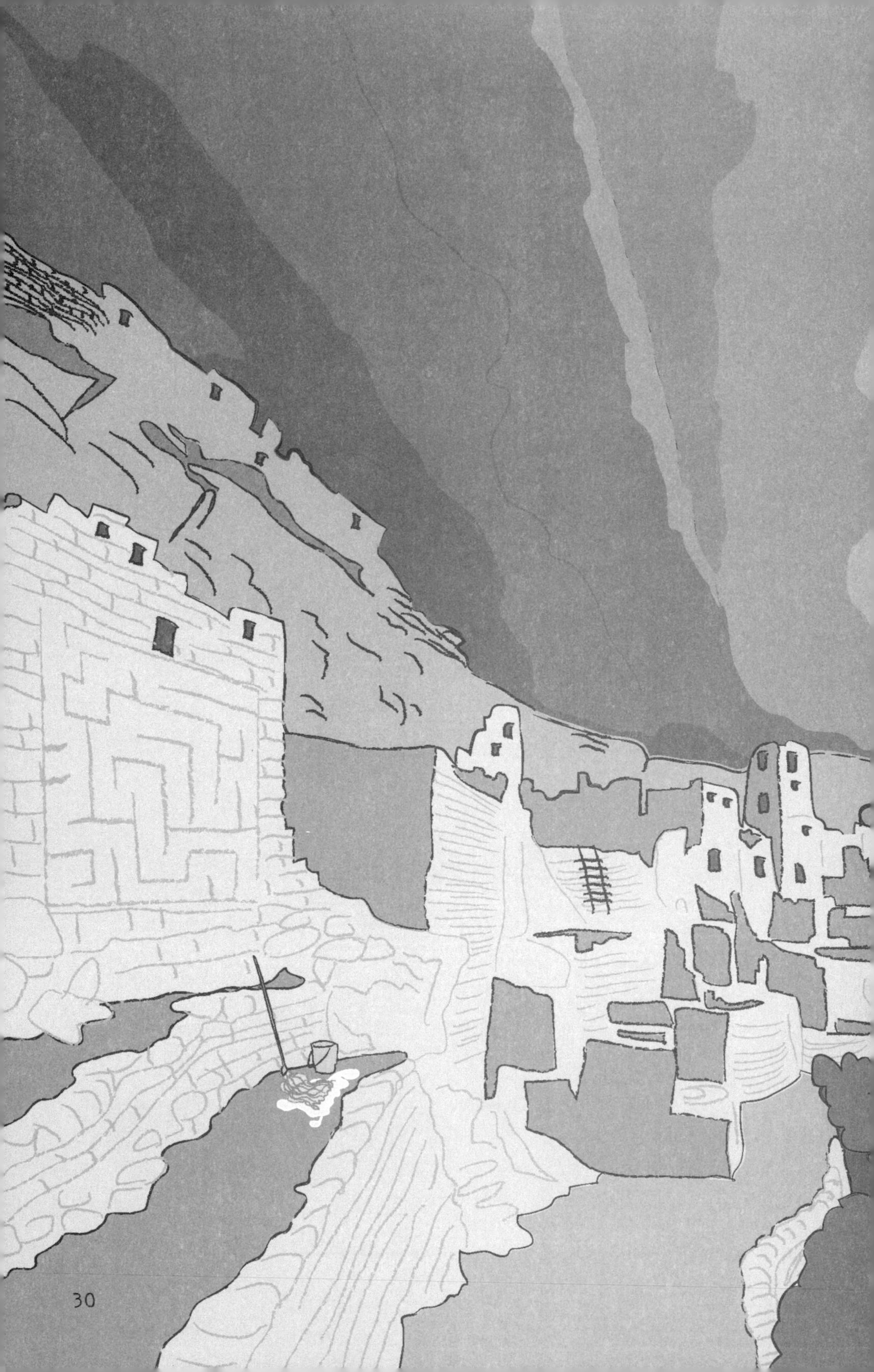

CLIFF PALACE

Sunburn-wise, it was a good thing the sun had dropped behind the mesa. In fact, it was time for our Twilight Tour of Cliff Palace. First of all, Cliff Palace is, like the name says, a ginormous cliff fort—the biggest at Mesa Verde park. It has 150 rooms and a <u>bunch</u> of kivas. A hundred people lived there hundreds of years ago.

"What happened to the couches?" I asked, looking around at rock, rock, and more rock.

"The Ancestral Puebloans mostly sat on stone benches and the ground," said our tour guide, who was dressed in a cowboy costume, even though Halloween is 4 months away. "And they slept on the ground too, with blankets and sheepskin rugs."

I thought back to the naked scenes in the museum's glass cases. The guy was right. I'd noticed blankets and woven mats, but no upholstery. Bummer.

"Life was a heck of a lot harder then," Mrs. Shoemaker said. "Finding enough food and water, and keeping warm and dry, took up pretty much all their time. They had to work their fingers to the bone just to survive."

"I could do it," Marvin said. He held up his notebook. "I am Prepared, remember?"

"Totally manageable,*" I agreed maturely, even though I could not imagine anything more horrid.

"Good," Mom said. "Because tomorrow our real wilderness adventure begins."

Real wilderness? I didn't know what she was talking about, but I did not like the sound of it. I pasted on a mondo* smile anyway, because that's what Marvin was wearing.

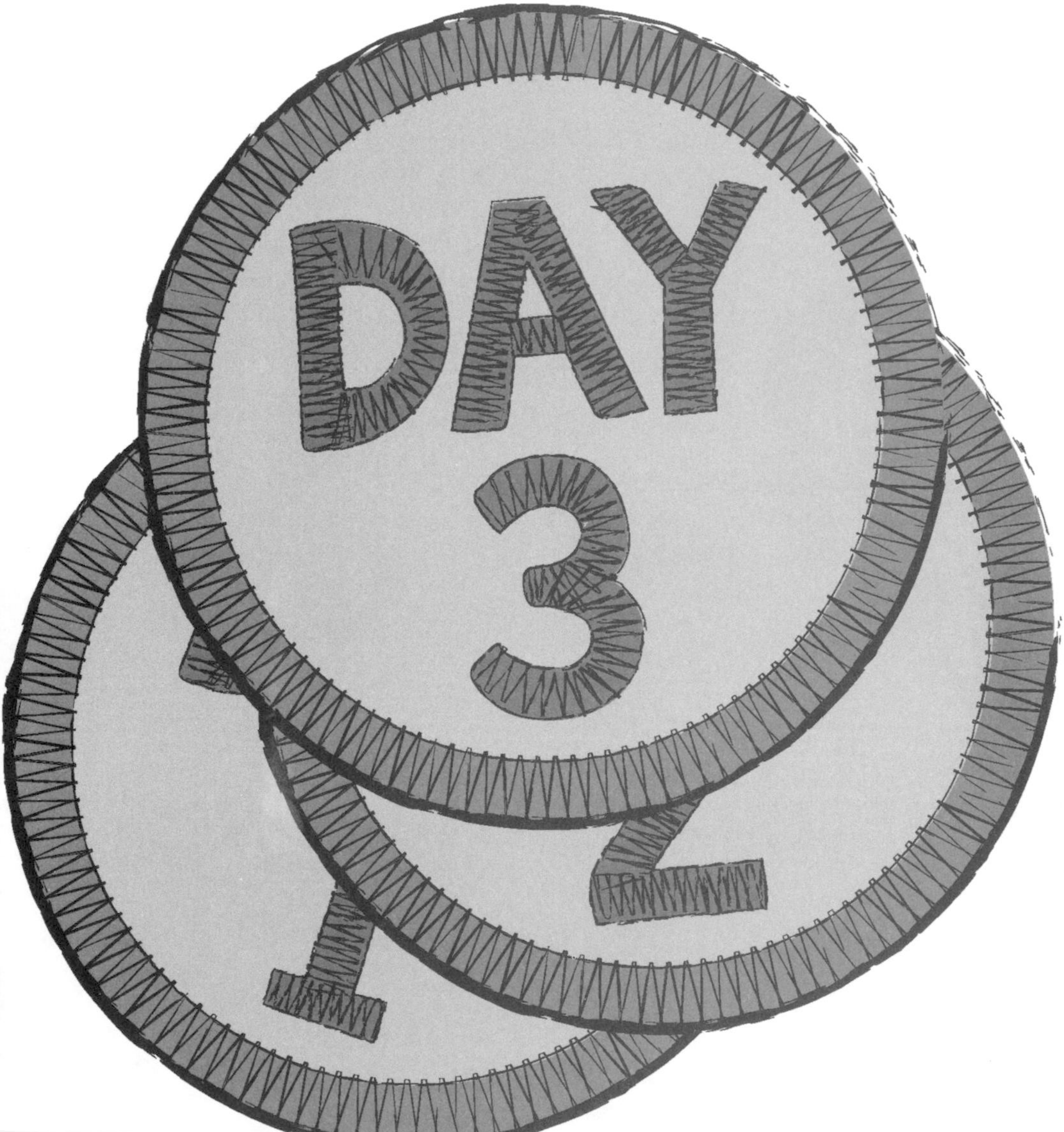
DAY
3

FOUR CORNERS

This morning we got up early, packed up our tents and other gear at Morefield Campground, and climbed back into the minivan. We drove for an hour to the exactly bottom-left corner of Colorado—a spot in the middle of flat, flat nowhere called Four Corners. It's marked on the ground and shows where the corner of Colorado forms a pie with the corners of 3 other states.

Marvin and I and Mrs. Shoemaker and my mom each stood in a different state, but we were still so close together that we could've reached out and touched each other.

MARVIN! LOOK ALIVE! WE'RE TRYING TO HAVE A MOMENT HERE!

35

"How's Arizona?" I asked Marvin, but he was busy scribbling in his notebook.

Max was lying down smack in the middle of the X on the ground, so he was in 4 states at once. He panted in the sun and heat. "Max needs water," I maturely pointed out.

"Yes, I'm glad you noticed," said Mom. "Actually, Aldo, I want you to be in charge of making sure Max has enough to drink for the rest of the trip. Here's a collapsible bowl." She handed me a blue fabric bowl-thingy. "Please keep this in your backpack and carry enough water for both of you at all times. I'll give you a second water bottle for him. Every time you take a drink, pour Max a drink too."

THIRST•E•MUTT

"I'd expect Max needs 1 to 2 liters of water a day," added Mrs. Shoemaker. "That's about a big plastic soda bottleful."

My tongue itched to complain. As I believe I've mentioned, water is heavy. But Marvin was writing all this down in his notebook, and Max was smiling up at me with his "Hero boy, you're-the-best-person-who-ever-lived" look. Plus, my brain reminded me, I'm a mature outdoorsperson now. So I poured some water from my bottle into his hiking bowl, and he lapped it up.

Then it occurred to me: Marvin would help carry water for Max if I asked him to, since Scouts are not only good campers, they're also good-deed doers. I'd hit him up later, when the moms weren't listening. I reached out to give him a high-5. "Gotta be Prepared, am I right?" I said.

"Yep," he answered. "We must dot the flies and cross the bees."

"Ohhkaaay...," I said. I had no idea what he was talking about, but it didn't matter. All that mattered was that my new buddy Marvin was going to come in handy.

AT THE TRAILHEAD

After Four Corners we drove for a couple more hours, to Manti-La Sal National Forest, in Utah. That's the state on the left side of Colorado.

"Here we are!" said Mom. She spread her arms wide and grinned like a madwoman.* "Our home for the next 3 days!"

MISERY*

I looked around. I didn't see any homes. I also didn't see any stone forts or campgrounds or cafés or all-you-can-eat pancake breakfasts. All I could see were miles of pine trees and rocky-red cliffs dropping down to a deep valley.

Mom reached up to pop open the storage pod on the roof of the minivan. She and Mrs. Shoemaker pulled out 4 ginormous backpacks.

"Here you go," Mom said, handing me a bright-orange behemoth bigger than Max.

"Um, I've got one," I said, looping my thumbs through the straps of the backpack I was already wearing.

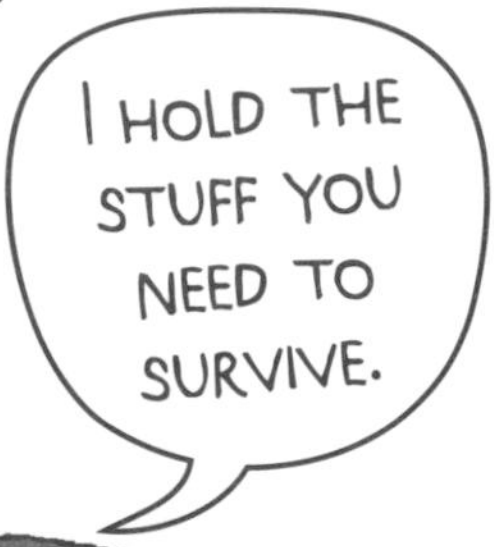
I HOLD THE STUFF YOU NEED TO SURVIVE.

"That's your daypack," Mom said. "This is your frame pack.

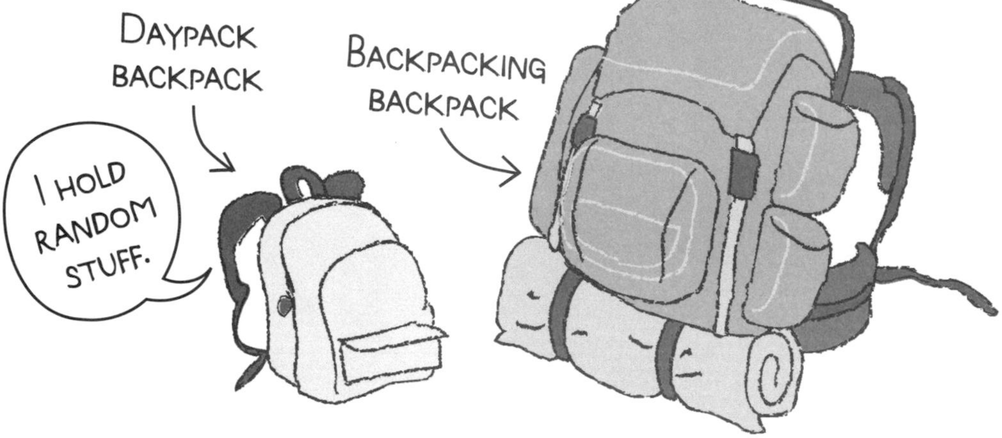
DAYPACK BACKPACK
BACKPACKING BACKPACK
I HOLD RANDOM STUFF.

"I've already loaded it with your sleeping bag and a few other essentials," she continued. "There's empty space at the top. Just make sure you have everything you need in your daypack, then tuck your daypack inside the frame pack. And off we go!"

"We're heading into the national forest, and we'll be hiking trails and camping along the way," she said. "3 nights. 4 days. So we have to carry everything we need."

By now Marvin had on his blue frame pack. It was almost as big as he was, but that didn't stop him from sprinting around like he was on fast-forward while the rest of us were on normal.

"OK, everyone," Mom said. "Mosquitoes are the most common native bird in these parts, so stand still and close your eyes and mouth." She sprayed each of us with mosquito repellent, head to toe. "Now. Are we ready?"

"One sec. I've gotta get a couple things," I said. I climbed back into the car and opened my daypack. I pulled out some stuff I wouldn't need, like my laptop and other miscellaneous junk, but there was one thing my daypack didn't contain yet, and that was my pillow. Pillows are <u>life.</u> So I tried to stuff it into my daypack, and when it wouldn't fit, I took out a few other random things to make room for it. Then I said goodbye to the minivan— my last tie to civilization—put my daypack inside my frame pack, and hoisted my frame pack. Imagine strapping a piano to your back and you'll have the idea. It was so heavy I almost turtled.

Mrs. Shoemaker laughed. "You'll get used to it," she told me.

IT'S NOT FUNNY.

"Pffft. This measly* thing?" I said. So far on this trip I was proving myself to be at least as good of an outdoorsperson as Marvin, and I wasn't about to admit defeat.

Finally, Mom put doggy hiking boots on Max so his feet wouldn't get cut up on the trail, attached his leash to his collar, and we started walking...

INTO THE WOODS

...And walking. And walking. We walked down a rocky hill, through a bunch of trees, and across a grassy meadow. Despite the mob of mosquitoes that buzzed within inches of our heads, the moms kept oohing and aahing at all the naturey stuff. Wildflowers! Bugs! Clouds!

I did not say, "Um, we have flowers and bugs and clouds in our own backyards..." because Mountain Man Marvin had joined in the oohing and aahing and was starting to write down each kind of wildflower and bug and cloud as the moms identified them.

HOW TO USE A WATER PURIFIER

☑ 1. FIND WATER. FLOWING is BEST.

☑ 2. PUT HOSE INTAKE INTO SOURCE.

☑ 3. ATTACH OUTPUT TO CONTAINER.

☐ 4. PUMP.

☐ 5. FLUSH AND CLEAN.

When we stopped at a stream to fill our water bottles, Mom showed us how to use a pump purifier, and she told us more about the Mexican Spotted Owl, which is the rare bird she hopes to see and take pictures of. "This specific forest is one of the owls' largest habitats," she said. "It's nesting season, so maybe we'll even get lucky enough to spot a whole family— a mom, a dad, and babies."

"How do we find them?" Marvin asked.

"We keep our eyes peeled," said Mom. "They hunt at night, but we might be lucky enough to see one sitting on a branch during the daytime. We should also look for nests and listen for their call. They sound like this..." Mom made a weird noise like a mixture of an owl's hoot, a dog's bark, and a chimpanzee's chatter.

Mom's birdcall made Max freeze like a statue and cock his head.

"I thought it'd be fun to have a contest," Mom said. "I brought a prize for whoever finds the first Mexican Spotted Owl."

"What's the prize?" I asked.

"A slingshot," Mom said.

I stopped and put my hands on my hips. "A little-kid-toy slingshot or a real slingshot?"

"A real slingshot," Mom said.

"I want it," Marvin said. He looked at me.

"I want it," I said. I looked at him.

"Good," Mom said with a conniving grin. "A little competition can be a productive thing."

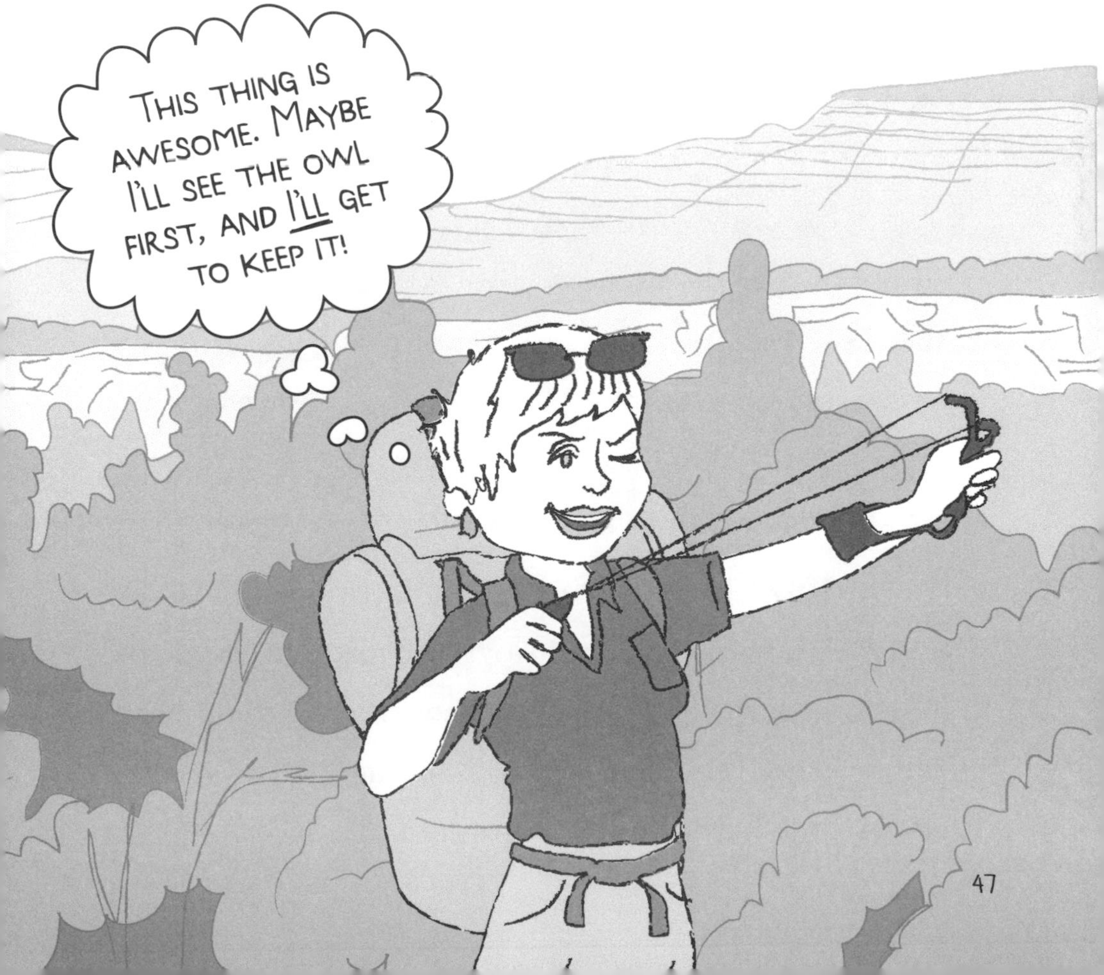
THIS THING IS AWESOME. MAYBE I'LL SEE THE OWL FIRST, AND I'LL GET TO KEEP IT!

LIONS & ELKS & BEARS
(OH MY)

We walked deeper and deeper into the wilderness, single file on the narrow trail—Marvin's mom in the lead, then me, then my mom and Max bringing up the rear. I was the filling in a mom sandwich, so I couldn't slow down or whine. To keep my mouth occupied, I started to whistle a tune instead.

Meanwhile, Marvin zig-zagged around us like a fly at a picnic, darting off the trail to check out plants and tree trunks and who knows what then zipping back to sync up with the mom sandwich before flying off again.

And even though this backpack was the heaviest thing I'd ever strapped to my actual body (versus my virtual body, because in Minecraft I can carry 40 slots of enchanted golden apples plus a full suit of gold armor, or a total of 119 million pounds—not like it's a big deal or anything), the walking seemed a little easier now because at least my eyes and my ears had something interesting to look for. That sneaky owl had to be hiding somewhere...and I was going to be the one to find it. So as we ambled, I eyeballed every branch and tree trunk, looking for a brown owl shape to reveal itself to me against the brown bark shapes.

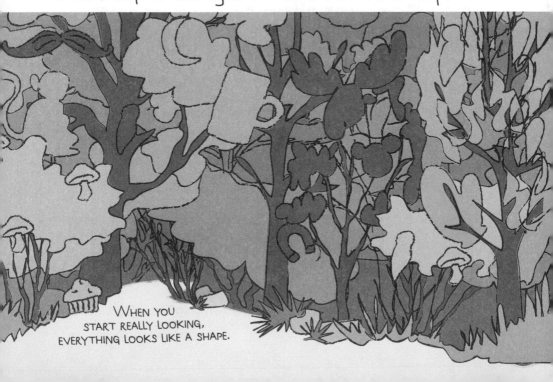

WHEN YOU START REALLY LOOKING, EVERYTHING LOOKS LIKE A SHAPE.

After a while Marvin started to get ahead of us, but his mom called him back. "We need to stay together!" she yelled. "We don't want anyone to get lost. And we have to be careful of bears and mountain lions!"

"Cool," I said casually, pretending that the fact we were in MORTAL DANGER* wasn't making the stubbly hairs on the back of my neck stand up. "I'll get some pics of them too."

"Do you boys know what to do if you see a mountain lion?" my mom asked. She stepped off the trail and into a shady area near some big boulders. She took off her pack, and we did the same. Rest break!

"Run away," Marvin said in answer to Mom's question. He climbed onto a boulder then jumped off it. On, off. On, off.

"No," Mrs. Shoemaker said sternly. "If you run away from a mountain lion, she'll think you're prey. She'll pounce on you and eat you for lunch."

"Speaking of lunch...," I said.

My mom dug into her pack and pulled out muffuletta* sandwiches for each of us. "If you see a mountain lion," she continued, "stop moving. Make yourselves look bigger by grouping together and raising your arms in the air. Make noise. Yell and shout. You want to look menacing.*"

LET ME KNOW WHEN YOU'RE DONE WITH YOUR LITTLE MASQUERADE.*

"Also," said Marvin's mom, "DO NOT look away. DO NOT turn your back."

"But what if the mountain lion keeps, you know, coming <u>toward</u> us?" I asked. My voice was thick with lunchmeat and foreboding.

"I put a can of bear spray in each of our daypacks," Mom said. She reached into her bag and pulled out a metal can about the size of silly string. "If a bear or mountain lion gets too close, just hold the can out in front of you, like this, and pull the trigger. It will spray a cloud of strong, peppery gas. Lions and bears don't like it. They'll usually go away."

I slid my hand into my mom's pack for a second sandwich. Usually, she'd said. I'd committed to being a great outdoorsperson, but I hadn't realized I'd be putting my life on the line! Sheesh. We all chewed in silence for a while. The quiet made the sound of something crashing through the woods behind us seem even louder. We jumped up and clumped together.

My mom held her bear spray can out in front of her. Milquetoast* Marvin grabbed my arm.

Out from the trees ambled a massive lady-elk. Whew. I'd met elks before. They're harmless. I shook off Marvin's hand and slid my phone from my pocket to take one of my famous wildlife pics.

"'Sup, elk," I said. She raised her head and laid her ears back, posing for me. She was about 3 minivan-lengths away. I took a step toward her to get a close-up.

"Stop," Mrs. Shoemaker whispered. "Back away slowly. She's upset."

I thought the elk seemed regular, but I shuffled backward anyway. Max, still leashed, growled. Then the elk shook her head and stamped the ground with a front foot. She was as big as an elephant, if an elephant had skinny legs and brown fur.

"Spray her!" I urged my mom. I was starting to come around to Mrs. Shoemaker's way of thinking.

"I don't want to hurt her!" Mom whispered back.

"It's her or your own child!" I pointed out.

Just then another creature wobbled into the clearing. It was an elk baby—dark brown like its mama, but with white spots. The baby rubbed up against the mom, and the mom reached her head down, stuck out her weirdly long, pale-pink tongue, and licked the baby's nose. Like, right across the nose holes. *Slurp.*

I got a few good photos before the elks turned their tan, fuzzy butts to us and bounded up the hill and out of sight.

"Wow," said Mrs. Shoemaker.

"Wow is right," said Mom.

"Is there an elk badge?" said Marvin.

"Did she just eat her baby's boogers?" I said rather unmaturely. "Cuz that's just disturbing."

LOOK OUT BELOW!

We death-marched another hour or 5 after the elk incident, with me doing a lot of owl-searching, slingshot-imagining, mosquito-slapping, and just-plain-whistling. When we finally stopped to make camp for the night, I unclipped my frame pack and let it fall to the ground, then I fell to the ground. My mosquito fan club followed me. Marvin jettisoned his pack and instantaneously climbed the nearest tree.

OH HORIZONTAL GROUND AND NOT MOVING, HOW I'VE MISSED YOU!

"Good job, guys," Mrs. Shoemaker said. "We got in about 5 miles today!"

"Well, usually 5 miles is a cinch for me," I said maturely, "but when you're carrying 50 pounds on your back, it seems a mite* farther."

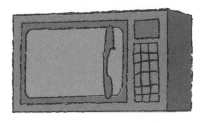

50 POUNDS

"I weighed our packs before we left home," Mom said as she began setting up the mom tent. "Yours is about 15 pounds, Aldo."

"Oh of course...that's what I meant, dear Mother...15. Come, Marvin, we have tent responsibilities to attend to."

15 POUNDS

Once our tent and bedding were ready, I desperately wanted to take a nap, but instead I gave my pillow a goodbye hug then climbed out of the tent and filled Max's water bowl. Next Marvin and I were sent to collect firewood. Those of you who know me might remember that I do not enjoy menial* tasks, but once again I set to whistling instead of grousing.

"Stay within sight of camp," Mrs. Shoemaker cautioned. "And stay together. We're on the buddy system now. Don't go anywhere by yourself, OK? Keep your daypacks on so your bear spray will be handy."

When Marvin and I were finally out of earshot of the moms, I exploded. "Backpacking is child abuse!" I said. "I mean, we're being forced to walk for miles and perform manual labor.* We're swarmed by disease-ridden mosquitoes. And we could be attacked by a bear or mountain lion at any second!" I have to admit, it felt really good to complain for a minute—like letting loose some epic flatulence you've been muscling in all day long.

WHEW! YOUR ATTITUDE STINKS! OH WAIT, THAT'S ME.

Marvin stooped to pick up another stick for the fire. "I disagree," he said. "It is fun. And social."

"Social? We're the only humans for mi—"

"Shhhh..."

I spun around, thinking we were about to be lion meat. I didn't see any predators, but now I heard what Marvin had heard. It was that owl-dog-chimp bird sound my mom had made.

Marvin dropped his armload of sticks and dashed off in the direction of the noise. "Hey!" I called after him. "No fair! You can run faster than me! Buddy system!"

But by the time I caught up to him, he'd already turned around to head back toward me. "I could not find it," he said. "It stopped hooting."

"Oh! Dang." Relief gushed through me. "Welp, we'd better get back or the moms will freak. Hey, this extra water I've been carrying for Max is kinda heavy. Wanna help?" I handed Marvin the Max bottle from my daypack.

"Sure." He took it and sprinted back to his twig pile.

I heard a familiar caw and looked up. A magpie perched on a branch overhead. I reached for my phone and held it up to take another photo.

"'Sup, magpie," I said. "Are you my mascot or what?"

By way of reply, a big black blob plopped onto my forehead and slid down my cheek. Yes, my mascot animal manured.* On my face.

"Grohhhhhhhsssss! How is that supposed to protect or guide me, you evil miscreant*?!"

He didn't answer. He just flew away, per usual. I wiped my face with the bottom of my shirt, closed my eyes, and slowly counted to 237.

This wilderness thing, it's merciless.*

DINNER AND A CAMPFIRE

Back at camp, Marvin and his marvelous pile of sticks already had a fire crackling. Mom and Mrs. Shoemaker chatted with their heads bent over a map.

"Are we gonna hike far tomorrow?" I asked as mellowly* as I could.

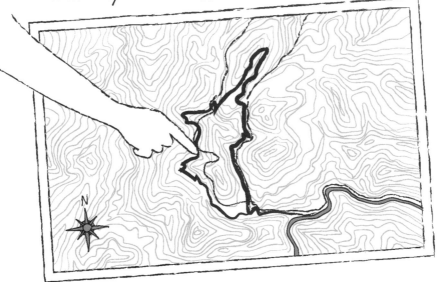

"Come look. Here's the route," Mom said, pointing at the map. "We started here. Here's the trail." She ran her finger over the paper. "The trail runs parallel to this creek, so we should have easy access to water. We'll pass by Ancestral Puebloan ruins here...and here...We'll loop by this canyon and that mesa, then in a couple days, we'll end up back at the minivan!"

"So...how long <u>is</u> the trail? Just curious."

"About 17 miles altogether, including our jaunts to the ruins. Are you hungry?" Now she was getting out the miniscule* backpacking stove to cook dinner.

"Yes!" I said. "I could eat a horse!"

"Me too!" she said. "Everyone has 3 freeze-dried dinners in their daypacks. So pick the one you'd like tonight, and I'll heat water to prepare them."

Oh yeah... I vaguely remembered Mom saying something back at home about prepackaged meals that were lightweight because all the moisture* was sucked out of them.

MARVIN'S LIST

HOW TO MAKE BACKPACKING FOOD
☐ 1. OPEN PACKET
☐ 2. POUR IN HOT WATER
☐ 3. STIR
☐ 4. WAIT 9 MINUTES
☐ 5. EAT RIGHT OUT OF PACKET!
☐ 6. PACK TRASH BACK TO CIVILIZATION

WHAT MARVIN'S LIST <u>DOESN'T</u> TELL YOU IS THAT BEFORE IT'S COOKED, BACKPACKING FOOD LOOKS LIKE THE STUFF IN THE DUSTPAN AFTER DAD SWEEPS THE KITCHEN FLOOR.

Since I'd already taken my pillow out of my daypack, it was pretty empty. I watched Marvin pull a blue, rectangular packet from his daypack.

"Mexican rice and chicken," he said, handing it to my mom.

"Pasta primavera!" said Mrs. Shoemaker, passing along her blue package.

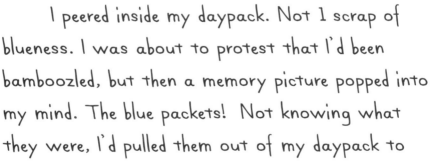

"Lasagna with meat sauce for me," Mom said. "Aldo?"

I peered inside my daypack. Not 1 scrap of blueness. I was about to protest that I'd been bamboozled, but then a memory picture popped into my mind. The blue packets! Not knowing what they were, I'd pulled them out of my daypack to make room for my pillow. My dinners for the next 3 nights were back in the minivan. My daypack now contained just 1 food item: a bag of marshmallows.

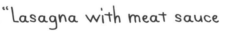

I pressed my palms to my eyeballs because crying is not mature. I didn't get a lecture, but I didn't get a hot dinner either. Mom mumbled something about "natural consequences" and handed me beef jerky and dried mangos. In between bites, I whistled. Mournfully.*

Soon it was dark, and the sky spangled with stars. I could see the North Star that the Mesa Verde park ranger had pointed out. We impaled marshmallows on sticks and charred them in the campfire. My belly finally full, I leaned against the log that was my chair and sighed. At least the mosquitoes had gone to bed for the night.

"I was just thinking about how you boys will be starting middle school in a couple of months," Mrs. Shoemaker said. "That's a big transition. Did you know that many Native American cultures sent boys about your age alone into the wilderness for several days on vision quests?"

"What's that?" I yawned.

"They were rites of passage into manhood," she explained. "The boy would eat nothing and pray to the spirits to have a vision—like a special dream or daydream that helped him find his purpose in life."

"My purpose is to be an Eagle Scout," Marvin said.

"If I didn't eat for a few days, I'd <u>definitely</u> have hallucinations," I said. "Wait—isn't it uber dangerous to leave a kid alone in the wilderness? Did they at least have bear spray?"

Mom chuckled and, before I could warn her, planted a kiss on my forehead, smack-dab in the magpie-poop zone. "It was normal in their culture," she said. "Remember, these were kids who essentially lived their entire lives outdoors."

After marshmallows, it was time for more menial chores.

MARVIN'S LIST

HOW TO GET READY FOR *Bed*, CAMP—STYLE
- ☐ 1. WASH UP, BRUSH TEETH
- ☐ 2. PUT FOOD, TRASH + SMELLY STUFF IN BAG
- ☐ 3. HANG BAG IN TREE— AWAY FROM BEARS!
- ☐ 4. DOUSE FIRE, STIR TILL COLD
- ☐ 5. LIGHTS OFF TILL TENT ZIPPED— NO BUGS!

BUT I'M HUNGRY!

ME TOO, BIG GUY. ME TOO.

The moon rose. Our eyelids started to fall. After we'd done all the stuff and slid into our sleeping bags, Marvin said to me, "I just remembered my other purposes: slingshot and people."

"Ohhhkaaayyy..." I couldn't see his face in the dark, but his voice sounded matter-of-fact,* like he was reading from 1 of his lists. The kid is definitely a mystery. We fell asleep to the snap of our tent fly in the wind and, somewhere in the distance, the faint but distinct hooting of an owl.

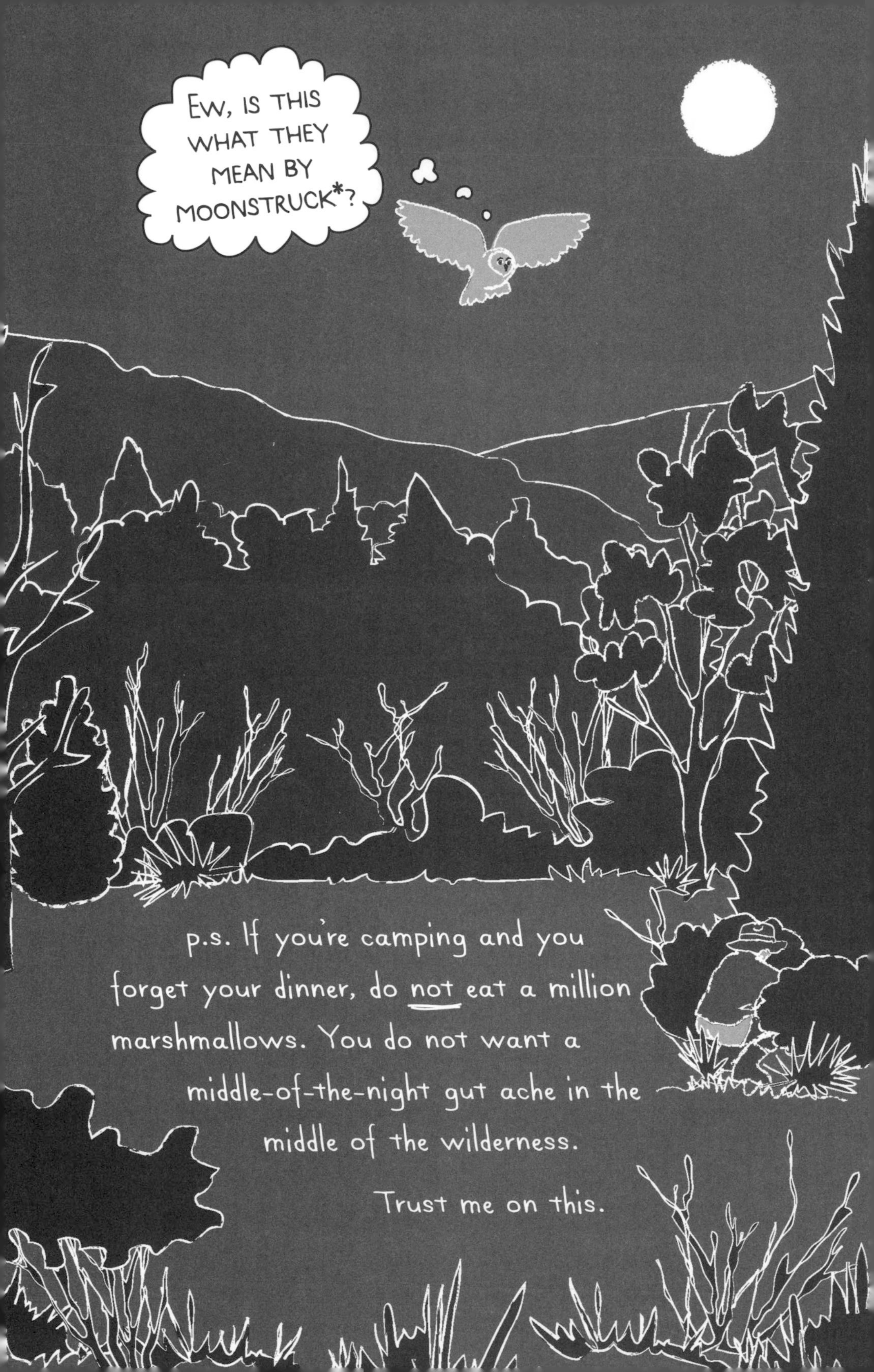
EW, IS THIS WHAT THEY MEAN BY MOONSTRUCK*?
p.s. If you're camping and you forget your dinner, do not eat a million marshmallows. You do not want a middle-of-the-night gut ache in the middle of the wilderness.
Trust me on this.

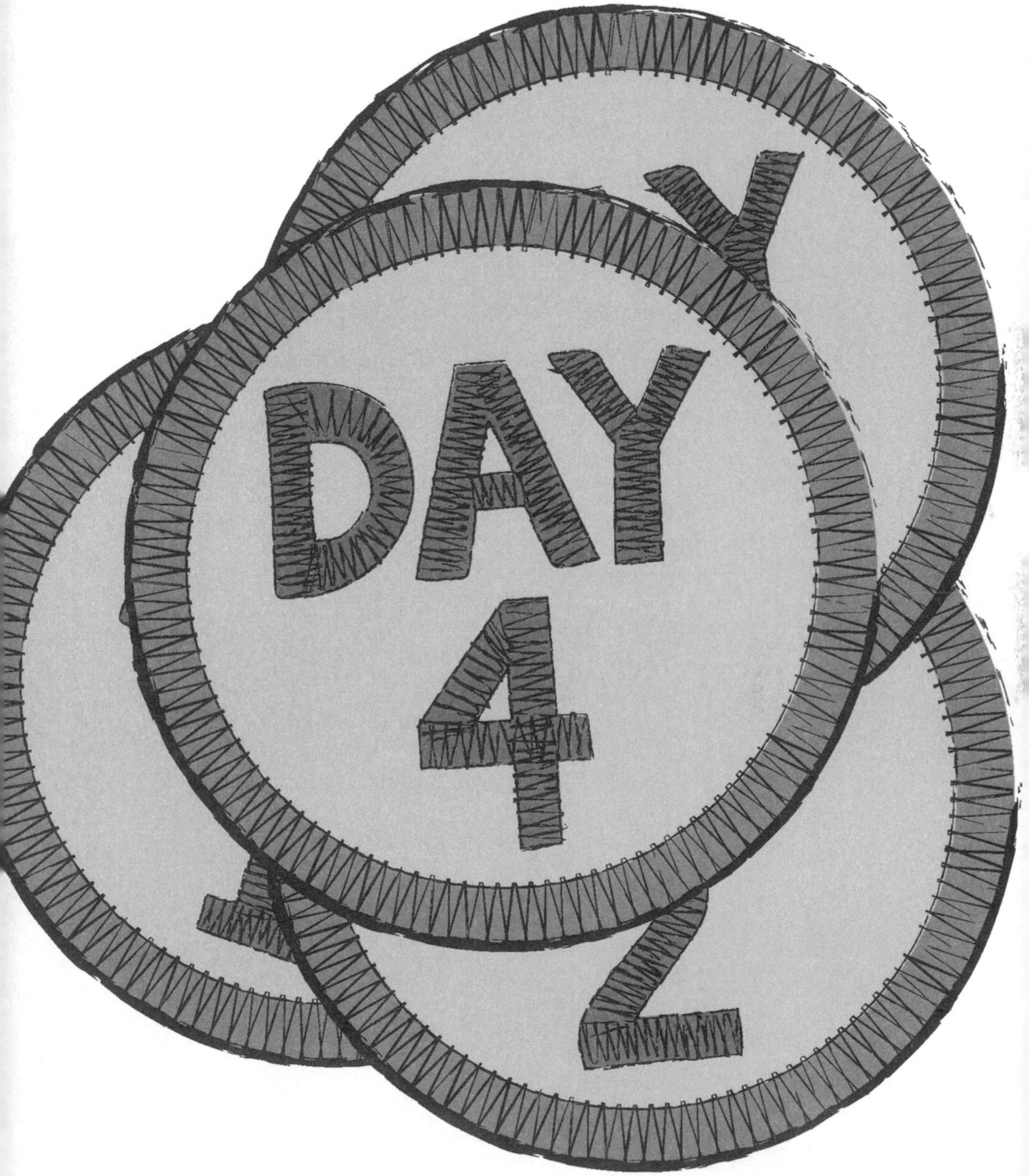
DAY
4

IT HURTS
SO BAD

I awoke to Max's moist* tongue on my forehead—again with the magnetic* poop zone!—and crawled from the tent into the blaring sun of a new day. I pulled on my shoes, stood, and stretched. That's when I realized that everything hurt. As in, everything. My shoulders ached. My face smarted. My feet throbbed. All my parts and pieces played a symphony of misery.

I tugged on my hat and looked around. Marvin and the moms swayed in the shade of a clump of nearby trees.

"Come join us, Aldo!" called Mrs. Shoemaker. "We're stretching out the stiffness. It's a magnificent morning!"

I minced* my way over to them and, remembering my indefatigable maturity, mustered a sorta-smile. A coating of bug spray, a few yoga moves, and a cup of hot chocolate later, I did actually feel better. The sun sparkled. The birds twittered. The breeze breezed. The Marvin packed up our tent.

After a skin-cancer lecture, Mom slathered me with sunscreen, and off we set. Once again I was the filling in the mom sandwich while Marvin was the fly. I whistled and walked, walked and whistled. Hiking wouldn't be so bad if you didn't have to move constantly.

Instead of my exhaustedness, I tried to think about Minecraft and the miracle of electricity and what summer-vacation merrymaking* Jack and Bee were probably up to at that very moment back home. Is this what grown-ups do all the time, I wondered— think about fun things while they're doing all the not-fun things they <u>have</u> to do?

Marvin flitted my direction. "Stop whistling," he demanded. His mom gave him a look. "Please," he added. "You are scaring the owls."

"How do you know?"

"Because I do not hear any owls."

I rolled my eyes skyward but did not argue. "Yes, Marvin, you are probably correct," I said a bit loudly, for the moms' benefit. "I shall cease immediately." Maturity points!

We hiked cattywampus down, down, down a cliffside. The moms identified more wildflowers, birds, and animal footprints. I took a few epic pics, and Marvin ran back and forth and made notes. We passed 2 hikers going the opposite direction, but they were the only other human life forms we saw.

The farther into the wilderness we went, the less green we encountered. There were fewer tall trees and grassy meadows and more pale-red rock and scrubby bushes that made my stomach moan* because they smelled like Thanksgiving stuffing. We were headed to the bottom of a canyon. Here and there, high above us, stone monoliths* shot into the sky. It reminded me of Mars. At least there weren't as many mosquitoes.

I THOUGHT WE'D SEE MORE HUMAN LIFE FORMS ON THIS TRIP.

BUT WE RAN INTO THE ZROSQAX'S! 34 MILLION MILES FROM HOME AND YOU SEE SOMEONE YOU KNOW... IT IS A SMALL SOLAR SYSTEM AFTER ALL!

When we were nice and sweaty, we stopped for a lunch break near some Ancestral Puebloan ruins. Even though they didn't have minivans, those ancient people sure got around.

We shrugged off our packs, and I rested in the shade while Marvin purified water from the stream, refilled our bottles, and gave Max a copious drink.

"We should climb up there," said Marvin, pointing to a cave tucked into the rock wall behind the ruin. It was maybe 15 feet off the ground.

I shook my head. "Too dangerous," I said. "Remember, safety first!"

"Owls nest in caves sometimes," he said. "I am going in."

I watched Marvin find bumps and cracks on the rocks to grab with his hands and push on with his feet. In seconds he'd slid the top half of his body into the cave, then his bottom half disappeared too.

"Welp, that happened," I said. I didn't want Marvin to find a Mexican Spotted Owl first, but I also didn't want to kill myself trying.

"He's a climber, all right," said Mrs. Shoemaker.

"Whoaaa!" It was Marvin's voice, all muffled* and echo-y. Then his face peeked over the cave's lip. "Aldo! You have to see this!"

I wasn't sure what the mature outdoorsman move was here. Was it better to remain safe on the ground, with the maternal units,* or climb up to the cave? I glanced sideways at Mom for a hint. But she wasn't looking at me; she was shielding her eyes with her hand and smiling caveward. And she wasn't warning me <u>not</u> to...

So I stepped to the wall and mimicked*
Marvin's climbing moves. I'm not gonna lie. It
was hard. I'm heavier than I look.
But in a jiffy there I was, deep
inside a pretty-dark cave in the
Utah wilderness with Marvin
Shoemaker. Maybe you're as
impressed with myself as I
was at that moment.

I'M NOT FAT.
I'M FLUFFY.

"What's the big
hairy deal?" I asked
Marvin.

He pointed at the ground. "No hair," he said.
"Just bones." It was a skeleton! He picked up the
skull. "Might be a...deer?"

I'M HEAVIER THAN I
LOOK TOO, YA KNOW.
I'M "BIG-BONED."

"Whoa! How does a deer
get into a cave like this?" I
grabbed my phone and took an
epic pic. "'Sup, skeleton," I said.

"Hmm. It would have to be
dragged up here by something really
strong... Something like a..."

We gawked at each other. Marvin's mouth fell agape. Together we whispered the only possible conclusion to his sentence: "...mountain lion!"

At first I was actually beating Marvin on the sprint-descent down the rock face, but as he was catching up, his left foot mooshed* my right hand. Ow! Instinctively I let go of my handhold, which made me flail backward. I grabbed Marvin's leg to steady myself. He claims that this pulled him loose from the wall, and we tumbled down the last couple of feet. This time I was the cushion and he was the cushioned.

Marvin popped up and ran over to the moms to show them the skull he'd filched. I could hear him recounting our adventure while I borrowed his first-aid kit to bandage my new scrapes and bruises. Did he give me a hand up? No, he did not. And did my mom minister* to my wounds? No, she did not. I was so miffed*!

Now I really hurt all over, outside and inside. But there was more pain yet to come.

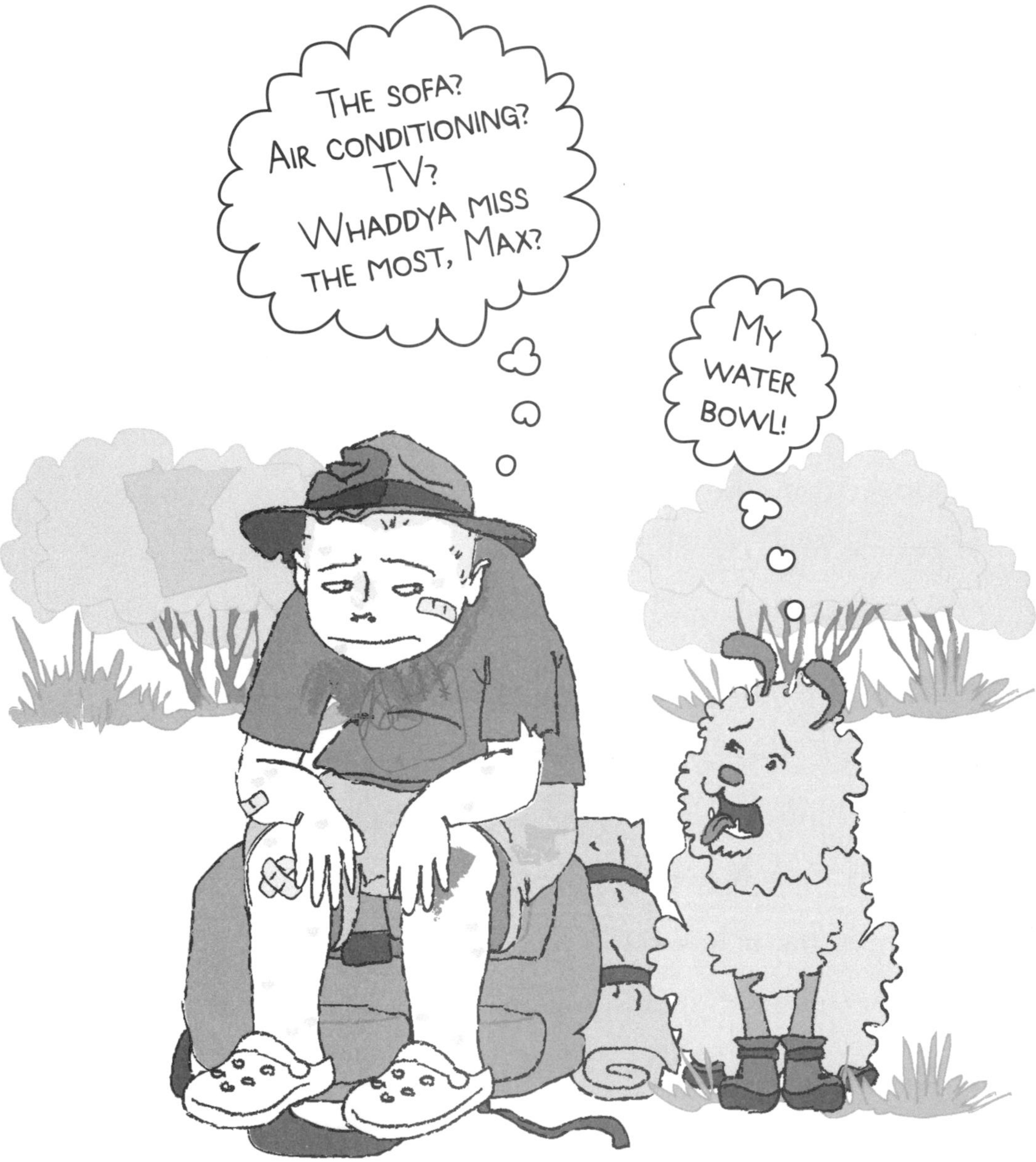
THE SOFA? AIR CONDITIONING? TV? WHADDYA MISS THE MOST, MAX?
MY WATER BOWL!

THE ANTS GO MARCHING

GUYS, WAIT UP! THIS CRUMB IS HEAVIER THAN IT LOOKS!

"Just another mile or so today!" called my mom from the front of the line. We were on the move again. Because it turns out that's what backpacking is: endless walking with a suitcase strapped to your mutilated* carcass.

By midday,* the amiable early-morning sun had become a malevolent* fireball, so when the afternoon clouds marshmallowed the sky, I was grateful. Yes, an influx of shade lifted my spirits a little, such was the appallingness of my circumstances.

Then it started to sprinkle. Now, I'm not a hygiene fanatic, but when you're tired and dusty, a gentle shower is like manna* from heaven. I tilted my head back and let the raindrops wash my face.

Marvin sprinted over and handed me a baggie of mouthwatering* macadamia nuts. I munched them as I hiked, and I was feeling so magnanimous* all of a sudden that I shared a few with Max. I snapped an epic pic of a rainbow in the distance. Maybe backpacking wasn't the worst thing after all...

But then the warm, meek* sprinkles turned to a cool, medium drizzle. Everyone stopped to get their rain jackets out of their backpacks. That's when I discovered mine was missing. Where was it? Likely, Mom said, back at the car with my freeze-dried dinners. Gah! I slipped on my sweatshirt instead.

I could feel my mood getting colder and darker too. Honestly, my maturity level was slipping. So after my mom led us in the "The Ants Go Marching" song, I belted out a new version I made up on the spot:

THE ANTS GO FARTING

THE ANTS GO FARTING 1 BY 1.
HURRAH, HURRAH.
THE ANTS GO FARTING 1 BY 1.
HURRAH, HURRAH!

THE ANTS GO FARTING 1 BY 1.
THE LITTLE ONE STOPS TO SMELL HIM SOME.

AND THEY ALL GO MARCHING DOWN, TO THE GROUND, TO GET OUT OF THE RAIN...

BOOM BOOM BOOM BOOM.
BOOM BOOM BOOM BOOM.

THE ANTS GO FARTING 2 BY 2.
THE LITTLE ONE STOPS TO DROP A DOO.

THE ANTS GO FARTING 3 BY 3.
THE LITTLE ONE STOPS TO TAKE A PEE.

THE ANTS GO FARTING 4 BY 4.
THE LITTLE ONE STOPS TO WIPE THE FLOOR.

ETCETERA. YOU GET THE IDEA.
(CAN YOU GUESS THE REST OF THE VERSES?)

I was definitely not being mature, but I couldn't help it! Every time I sang the next number of ants, Marvin burst out his bizarre, mulish* laugh, which made the moms guffaw, and before you know it, all 4 of us were singing my dumb farting song at the top of our lungs while marching in the rain. I'm guessing my brain was muddled* from the excessive physical activity and endless OUTSIDEness, but it was merry in a delirious sort of way.

Then the lightning flashed, and Mrs. Shoemaker shouted that we needed to take cover. I agreed, of course, because break time! So we ducked under a roomy rock overhang and settled in as it really started to pour. But even that was kinda-sorta, well, magical. Have you ever stood under the shelter of a porch while just a few feet away rain came down in buckets? It's like seeing an elk up close. The beauty of nature can surprise you, but it's the powerfulness of it that makes it so you can't turn away.

In between thunder booms, Mrs. Shoemaker
told jokes and shared her M&Ms. She passed
around lemonade powder, too, so we could turn
the plain old warm smelly-feet water in our water
bottles into liquid gold. Yum! Mom handed me a dry
sweatshirt to replace my wet one. She also fed
Max some dog treats she'd packed. Marvin tossed
me a water bottle and Max's bowl, so I could give
him a drink. We had a surprisingly fun little party
while we waited out the storm.

Until a mouse decided to crash the festivities!

The creepy critter must've been lured by the smell of our city food. It climbed onto my shoe and dashed up my leg. I howled and jumped up. I stamped my feet and wildly wiped my hands over my clothes, in case he was still attached. Everyone else screamed too and then started to laugh when they realized it was "just a mouse."

Unfortunately, in the melee* I let go of Max's leash, and he took off after the mouse, into the downpour. Then Marvin took off after Max. Then, because I didn't know what else to do— I took off after Marvin.

The thunder and the rain pounding the rocky canyon floor were already noisy, but we added to the cacophony. The moms were yelling at me, who was yelling at Marvin, who was yelling at Max, who was barking at the darting mouse. Lightning strobe-lighted the scene. It was mayhem*!

The canyon was only a minivan or 2 wide at that point, with steep rock walls on either side and a dinky stream running down the middle, except now the dinky stream rushed with rainwater. I saw that while we were partying it had doubled from a 2-foot-wide trickle to a 4-foot-wide, fast-moving creeklet.

Would a mouse jump into that maelstrom* to escape? Maybe so, because mice are supervillains. Regardless, Max must've thought that's where the mouse went because with a wild, running leap, in he plunged. The creek was deep enough now that Max had to swim, and I could see his legs churning madly while he struggled to keep his nose above water. And the current had him. He was being carried downstream!

Marvin was closer to Max. "Save him!" I yelled.

But Marvin probably didn't hear me because before the yell was even out of my mouth, he took his own wild, running leap and dove after Max. Max's leash was floating in the water, and Marvin grabbed it. Then I fell in. My hat got swept away, but Marvin didn't because my mass* accidentally anchored him. We managed to get to our feet in the knee-deep water, and with the moms clucking around us, we carried Max back to the party shelter together.

Don't worry—Max was completely fine. Everyone was completely fine. Yes, there was some lecturing about how dangerous floods are and how you should never, never, never enter swift water, but there were also lots of mom-hugs and exclamations about courage and matureness. And Marvin, even as I watched him get out his notebook to make a new list (Flash Flood Safety Tips), to me he seemed more regular somehow, like a normal-weirdo instead of a weird-weirdo. Someone you might hang around with sometimes.

Maybe.

MATURE IS ⒶS MATURE DOES

Minutes later the sun was back, because that's how the sun works in the part of the country where I live. It dried us as we hiked onward. We walked along the creek, which was already back to baby-stream status. The landscape was getting greener again. The mosquitoes were getting thicker again.

When we finally reached a grassy meadow with clumps of trees where Mom wanted to set up camp for the night, I lay down, still wearing my giant pack, and I closed my eyes.

I woke to a snapping campfire and my mom's outstretched hand handing me a steaming pouch of spaghetti and meatballs. I sat up, and she helped me take off my pack.

"Thanks, Mom," I said. "You're a nice mom."

"You're welcome," she said. "It's the least I can do to share my food with a hero." I knew I was an accidental hero, but I took the meal anyway.

"All's well that ends well," said Mrs. Shoemaker. "Right, Marvin?"

"Right," said Marvin. "Aldo is well in the end. Hey—a magpie!"

Sure enough, a magpie perched on a boulder near me. I clutched my spaghetti to my chest. "Go away!" I threatened, waving an arm.

JUST CHECKIN' IN!

He didn't budge, so I glared at him. Mascot, schmascot. The mooch wasn't getting 1 morsel of my exquisite dinner. And that's when I heard it...uber faintly. The owl-dog-chimp sound. I glanced at the others. They were busy masticating* and chatting. Marvin was scribbling in his notebook.

I set my dinner pouch on the ground and covered it with someone's jacket. "Just gotta use the lavatory real quick...," I said, and fake-calmly I ambled off.

The owl kept hooting, and I could hear myself getting closer, closer, closer, like it was giving me clues: "Warmer. Warmer. Warmer." And then there he was, hunkered down on a low tree branch, like it was no big deal. I took out my phone and snapped a close-up. "'Sup, Mexican Spotted Owl," I said.

The slingshot was mine! I backed away slowly then turned and ran to camp. But no one was there! I listened. I could hear footfalls. Fast ones.

"I found the owl!" said Marvin, running up to me. "Come see!" And before I could argue, he sped off again, in the opposite direction of _my_ owl.

I followed, livid fists clenched. The moms and Max and Marvin stood near a tall pine tree. Marvin pointed at a hole in the trunk. Perched on the lip of the hollow were 1 big owl and 3 smaller, whiter, fuzzier ones.

"Well that's great and all," I said measuredly,* "but I found one first...like 10 minutes ago." I whipped out my phone and showed my mom the indisputable evidence. Luckily, the photo even showed the exact time it was taken.

"Wow!" Mom said. Her eyes shone with owl adoration. "What a beauty! We're so lucky to be seeing all these owls!" Then she immediately resumed taking a billion photos of Marvin's owl family with her fancy camera.

Marvin crossed his arms in front of his Scout shirt.

"Where's the slingshot?" I asked Mom. "I think I'll go try it out."

"It's in the front pouch of my frame pack," Mom said. "But Aldo..."—and here she stopped taking pictures for a second so she could look me in the face—"your owl is a barred owl. They look really similar to the Mexican Spotted...but the barred owl has bars on the breast and streaks on the belly. Barred owls are also amazing, but they're relatively common."

WUT?

That's all Marvin needed to hear. He took off running again. And again I followed.

By the time I got to camp, he'd already retrieved the slingshot and was cocking a pinecone in its ammo pocket.

"I want it," I said.

"I won it, like a square at the fair," he said.

"Gimme it."

"No."

So for all the times Marvin Shoemaker had gotten on my nerves on this stupid trip, I tackled him.

We rolled around in the grassy area in the middle of the campsite, and I tried to pull the slingshot from his Hercules grip. I was heavier, but he was more athletic (the story of my life). He broke free and sprinted off.

OK, I hadn't been very mature, but at least I'd kept my words to myself. I hadn't said even <u>1</u> mean thing out loud.

That is, until I I realized that my dinner was now an inedible mess. It was smeared all over the jacket I'd used to hide it from the magpie plus the clothes I was wearing plus other unfortunate items that happened to be in the wrestling arena. At that point I <u>did</u> say a few mean things out loud. If an almost-middle-schooler swears in the woods but no one's close enough to hear him, did he really swear?

I peeled off my spaghettied clothes, zipped myself into the tent, and slid into my sleeping bag (which Marvin must've set up earlier, while I napped. Gah!). So what if I silently blubbered myself to sleep? You would have too.

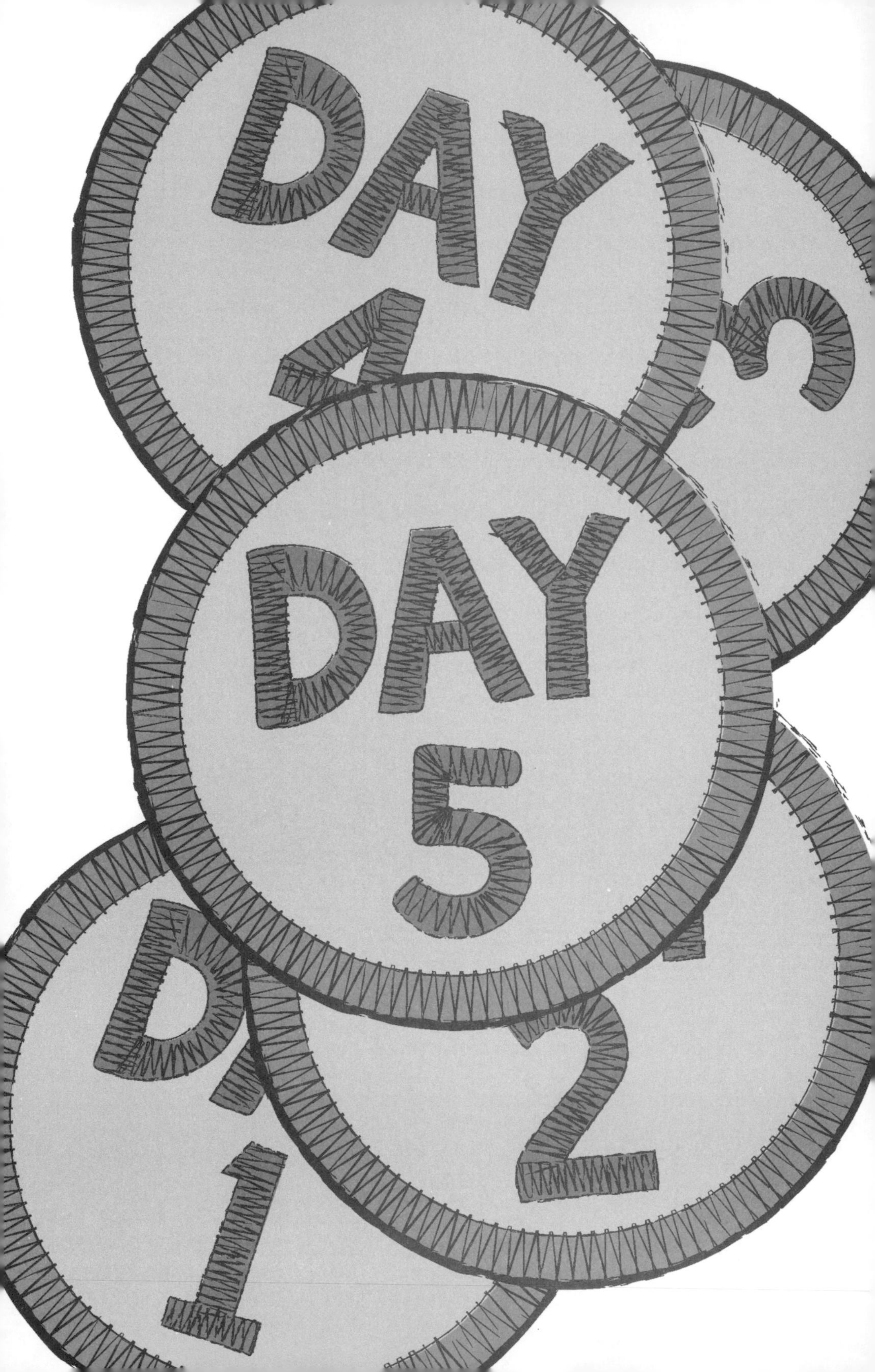
DAY
4
3
DAY
5
2
1

I AM SO DONE

I woke to the rumbling of a lawnmower, which after a couple disorienting seconds I realized was my own stomach. You know you're famished when your body organs start to audibly complain. On the floor of the tent, about 6 inches from my face lay Marvin's. He slept on, mouth-breathing* directly into my nose holes.

I pulled on the nearest clothes and unzipped the tent door. Immediately a mosquito army had me surrounded.

"Good morning, Aldo!" My mom's bright voice only irritated me further, but I tried to stay calm and mature, because I knew that calm and mature was the only chance I had for my new plan to succeed.

"Good morning, Mother." I kept my voice low, so as not to alert Marvin. "I would like to discuss something. Would you follow me, please?"

With Max on his leash, Mom and the mosquitoes followed me down the path, past some trees and around some large rocks. I stopped and turned to her.

I THINK IT'S TIME WE LOOKED AT THIS THING LIKE THE MATURE ADULTS WE ARE. WOULDN'T YOU AGREE, MOTHER?

"Now that we have been so fortunate as to observe the Mexican Spotted Owl," I said matter-of-factly, "I realize that we have completed our quest. I worry Max's paws may be getting sore, despite the hiking booties. Furthermore, Marvin has earned the slingshot, which means the contest has also run its course. Therefore, I'm sure you will agree with me that it is time to pack up our gear and make our way back to the trailhead. Alas, this memorable expedition is coming to its natural conclusion."

As I delivered my monologue,* Mom tilted her head and raised her eyebrows—her surprised-but-leery face. Finally she said, "I understand that you're finding this trip a challenge, and I'm proud of you for trying so hard. But we only have 1 more night. You can do it!"

Have you ever noticed that sometimes 1 more night is just plain out of the question?

I dropped my voice to a whisper. "I did not want to betray his confidence," I continued, flattening mosquitoes like a human flyswatter, "but Marvin has shared with me that he would like to return home. I believe his Scout group has an important meeting tomorrow morning, and he is quite distressed that he will miss it."

THINK SHE BOUGHT IT?

I KNOW I DID.

TOTALLY.

MOMS. THEY CAN BE HARD TO READ.

I know, I know. As lies go, it was a feeble one. But it was the best malarkey* I could come up with in that moment, malnourished* as I was. What do I look like, a mendacious* genius! Sheesh!

Mom put one hand on each of my shoulders. "You went to bed early last night," she said, her eyes shiny with motherliness,* "but Marvin sat with us at the campfire. He told us about the fight you 2 had, and I saw what happened to your spaghetti. After you apologize to him, I'll share my breakfast with you. You must be starving! How does that sound?"

Apologize to Marvin? Apologize! I accelerated from mature to meltdown in no time flat. "I'm done!" I screamed. "I Am So Done!" I ran back to the campsite and flung on my daypack. I spotted the slingshot, which was lying on the ground near the tent. I snatched it up.

Marvin was sitting on a rock, lacing up his hiking boots. "Where are you going?" he asked. "Why are you wearing my Scout shirt?"

"Mind your own wilderness!" Gah! Now I was the one who wasn't making any sense! I marched away and down the trail.

As I passed my mom, she said, "Aldo, stop. You can't wander off alone. It's dangerous."

"Fine. I'll take Max." I grabbed his leash from her and kept on marching. It was time to take matters into my own hands.*

TREES AND ROCKS
ROCKS AND TREES

But seconds later I heard those infuriatingly sprinty footsteps coming up behind me. I turned off the trail to escape them and went down a little hill and past a patch of sagebrush (that's the stuff that smells like Thanksgiving). Marvin found me anyway.

ALDO. ARE YOU AWARE THAT THIS SHIRT OF YOURS IS WRECKED? AND ALSO? IT SMELLS TERRIBLE.

YOUR MOM SAYS YOU HAVE TO GO BACK TO CAMP.

"I'm being a mature, non-moochy outdoorsperson," I said without breaking stride. "I'm going full mountain-man* status and hunting for my own food."

"Hunting what?" Marvin's voice was half curiosity, half admiration.

"A squirrel. Maybe an elk."

"You can hunt elk with a slingshot?"

"If you've got clutch aim. Which I do." I stooped to pick up an egg-sized rock and cocked it in the pouch of the slingshot. I let go and the rock pinged a tree on the next hill over.

We meandered* farther, up a different hill and around a tree clump. Not a mammal in sight. My anger was moderating,* but my hunger was multiplying. I glanced down at Max and saw he was panting.

"How do you cook an elk?" Marvin asked.

"With fire. Duh."

"But, how do you get the fur off?"

"I don't know! Don't you have a list for that?"

Marvin retrieved his notebook from his daypack. He flipped through it as we skirted a rock formation....

...and another Puebloan ruin and some more trees...

...and some more rocks and some more rocks...

...and some more trees, plus a bunch of cactus.

The scenery was starting to look a lot like a repeating cartoon background.

"No, I do not have a list for that," he said eventually. "Do not get blood on my Scout shirt. Please."

When I'd thought about hunting, I hadn't thought about the blood. I stopped. Max stopped. Marvin stopped.

"Let's sit down and watch for animals for a while," I said. I sat. Max sat. Marvin sat.

Marvin got out Max's bowl-thingy from my daypack and filled it with water from his daypack. Max drank and drank.

"So, what's on the snack menu?" I asked after a few minutes.

Marvin peered into his pack. "Beef jerky." He handed me a stick.

I devoured it. He gave me another.

"I do not see any animals," Marvin said. He was sitting, but his foot jiggled. He was getting impatient. He took a swig from his water bottle then passed it to me. "We should go back."

Thanks to the beef jerky, my hunger was mollified.* I was tired. Plus, who was I kidding? I couldn't hunt! I couldn't kill an elephant-sized animal with a rock! I didn't know the first thing about getting fur off of live meat! I sighed.

"OK, let's go back," I agreed.

We stood and turned around. We walked past the rocks and the trees and the trees and the rocks. We hiked for an amount of time that seemed longer than it should have.

"Where the heck did that Puebloan ruin go?" I asked in frustration. I stopped. I looked around. I squinted up at the sun high in the sky. I could feel my hatless head frying to a scalpy crisp.

"I do have a list for <u>this</u>," Marvin said.

"For what?

Marvin opened his notebook and held out a page for me to read. At the top, in bold letters, it said:

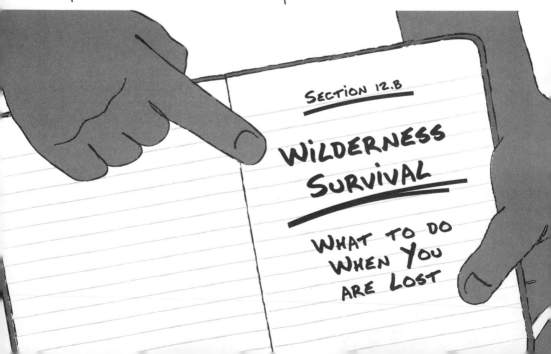

SECTION 12.8

WILDERNESS SURVIVAL

WHAT TO DO WHEN YOU ARE LOST

L-O-S-T

"We're not lost!" I said, though instantly I felt my insides twist. "We just made a minor mistake."

Marvin ignored me and searched his notebook. Finding a certain page, he said, "We should stop."

"We <u>are</u> stopped!"

"No." He showed me the word in the notebook. "We should S.T.O.P."

"Fine. Let's think. We ambled a little ways away from camp, and now we're going back. Easy peasy."

"Which way is camp?" Marvin asked.

"OK, you're the Boy Scout—we'll go your way," I said.

"Except I am not sure," he said. "When you are not sure, the list says stay put."

"Like, sit here?"

"Yes. So our moms can find us. If we move, we can get more lost."

Now normally I'm a sitting enthusiast, but at that moment I wasn't feelin' it. "How 'bout this," I said. "I'll go my way, and you go yours. Whichever one of us finds the moms first will come get the other one."

"The list says no splitting up," Marvin said. "Stay together. Buddy system."

I'd stayed together with this kid for 4 days solid already and what good had it done me? Max licked my hand, and I reached down to scratch his ear like I do. He whimpered.

"He is thirsty," Marvin said. He pulled the Max bottle from his daypack and held it up to the sunlight. It contained about 2 inches of water. Then he checked his own water bottle. It was half empty. "12 ounces of water, total" he said. "That is what I have." He arranged the remaining contents of his daypack on the ground and named them out loud. "Sunscreen. Rain jacket. Bear spray. Matches. First-aid kit. Water purifier. Pocket knife. Mirror. 2 beef jerkies. 1 protein bar. 1 freeze-dried meal. Whistle. Skull."

A SCOUT IS ALWAYS PREPARED.

A whistle! Never had I been so happy to see a plastic noise-making device. I grabbed it and blew. Silence. I blew harder. The only sound filling the air was Max's incessant panting.

Marvin took the whistle and inspected it. "It is cracked," he said matter-of-factly. "The ball part is missing. It might have broken when you fell on me."

When I scowled, my sunburn stung. "You fell on me, too, remember? Probably that's what broke it." I was getting flustered, but Marvin, he remained calm, cool, and collected.

"Try _your_ whistle," Marvin said, pointing at my daypack.

I peered at my pack's meager* contents.

UTILITY IS IN THE EYE OF THE PROBLEM-SOLVER?

But in the small front pocket, I still had...

"I may not have a whistle, but we can <u>call</u> our moms!" I shouted. Instantly, though, the upper-left corner of the screen mocked* me with those 2 terrible words: No Service. "GAHHH!"

Yet I could still hear hear my shout echoing off the rock walls around us. "Derp," I said. "We can just yell. We can yell louder than a whistle." I looked up at the sky to project my voice up and over the rocks and screamed, "HELP! HELP! HEEELLLP!"

Marvin joined in. "HEEELLLP!!!" It felt silly, bellowing like that, because we were fine. We weren't in immediate danger. And our moms were probably just a couple rock and tree clumps away. So why weren't they finding us? The possibility of being really and truly lost squeezed my heart.

We climbed to the top of a knoll so our voices would carry farther. Marvin jumped and waved his arms and shouted, and I followed his lead. When we were too tired to flail around anymore, Marvin got out his mirror and tried sending sun reflections in all directions. Meanwhile, we listened for whistle noises, in case our moms were blowing their whistles. We sat and we waited. We did everything the list said.

I stood on the hilltop and turned slowly in a circle. I could see for miles. Here's what I observed in every direction: hills, rocks, trees, and sky. It all looked the same. I couldn't find the stream. I couldn't spot any ruins. I couldn't even tell which direction was which because the stupid sun made it impossible for me to see the North Star.

I buried my face in Max's fur. He and I were lost in the hot, dry, middle of nowhere.* We were going to die of starvation then turn into a pile of bones just like the skeleton Marvin had found. And as I lay dying, Marvin Shoemaker would be the last human being I'd ever see.

THE FRUITS OF OUR LABOR

We climbed down from the knolltop and found some shade under a rock overhang. The mosquitoes, which had mostly left us alone on the breezy peak, took this opportunity to rejoin us.

"We need to make an emergency shelter," Marvin said with maddening* calmness. "In here."

"What for? To shelter our moldering* corpses?" I moaned and felt tears clog my eye sockets. I didn't even bother to slap at the mosquitoes. I just let them begin the inevitable process of chewing away my mortal* flesh. Max licked my sunburnt cheek, but his tongue felt like a dry towel. "I'm sorry, boy," I whispered.

"The shelter will keep us warm if it storms or gets windy," Marvin said. "And we can sleep in it. This is a good spot, but we have to collect branches to make a lean-to."

Marvin passed me his water bottle. I took 2 tiny sips, even though every molecule* in my body was begging me to gulp all of it. Marvin poured some water for Max. Then he stood, and he reached down and gave me a hand up.

"Pick up pebbles and put them in your pockets," Marvin instructed as he scooped stones.

I did as I was told. I was too melancholy* to argue. The stones made me think of all the times I'd been rock collecting with Jack. These memories weighed me down even more.

"We will head toward those trees over there." Marvin pointed. "We will drop a line of rocks while we walk. So we can find our way back to this spot."

"Like Hansel and Gretel," I mutter-blubbed. "Or don't you recall how that worked out for them..."

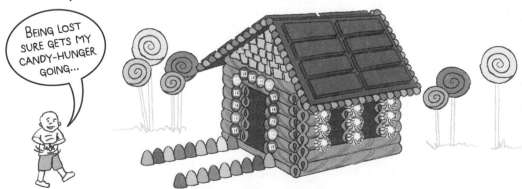

BEING LOST SURE GETS MY CANDY-HUNGER GOING...

At the clump of pines, we yanked some branches off a tree. It was grueling getting the tree to part with them, though, so we only got a small armload. Sticky with sap, we dragged them back to our shelter and propped them around the opening, making a sort of raggedy tent.

Marvin was smiling. "What's your deal?" I asked.

"I will get a survival badge," he said.

"Only if we survive!" I growled.

"We will," he said. I did not share Marvin's confidence, but I must admit, it made me feel a modicum* better.

Next we followed our rock line back out into the canyon. We went farther this time, breadcrumbing more pebbles as we walked. "We can survive without food for many days," Marvin said, "but we will need more water today."

I remembered what my mom had said: "You can't survive without water, Aldo. You have to carry it at all times on this trip." I don't know <u>why</u> she has to be so right all the time. Sheesh.

But water was nowhere to be found. Just more rocks and trees and mosquitoes and myriad* cactuses.

A COMEDY OF CACTUSES:

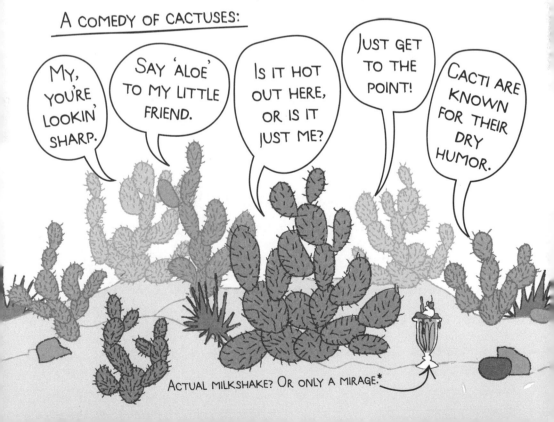

MY, YOU'RE LOOKIN' SHARP.

SAY 'ALOE' TO MY LITTLE FRIEND.

IS IT HOT OUT HERE, OR IS IT JUST ME?

JUST GET TO THE POINT!

CACTI ARE KNOWN FOR THEIR DRY HUMOR.

ACTUAL MILKSHAKE? OR ONLY A MIRAGE.*

<u>Cactuses!</u> "Hey!" I said. "In that movie at the museum, the Ancient Pueblo guys ate cactus fruits. Like, the fruits gave them food <u>and</u> moisture, because they're juicy inside. The fruits—not the people." I looked more closely at the nearest cactus. No fruit—just green spikes.

We inspected more and more cactuses of all shapes and sizes and finally found a tall one with big leaves. Attached to some of the leaves were blobby greenish-red things shaped kinda like pears. To me it looked like flattened feet with swollen toes.

I reached out to grab one of the pears. "Ow!" I yelled and stuck my finger in my mouth. "It's full of sharp prickers!"

I wrapped the empty marshmallow bag around my hand, then I pulled the sock over the protective plastic. Insta-glove! I yanked down a pear. The fruit was now in our possession, but it was still covered with spikes. Marvin found a stick, sharpened it with his pocket knife, and plunged it into the fruit. Juice oozed from the hole. Jackpot! I high-5ed Marvin, and he grinned.

We tried holding the leaky fruit over our faces and catching the drips in our mouths, but that didn't really work. So Marvin used the stick as a handle while he carved off the spiky skin with his knife. Inside, the fruit was goopy magenta* flesh dotted with a million hard little seeds. We ate it anyway, seeds and all, then another, then another. The flavor tasted like watermelon mixed with bubble gum. It was definitely one of the tastiest non-meat foods I've ever eaten. The fruit filled my belly, too, but I was still thirsty.

And I couldn't get Max to eat any fruit at all. So Marvin and I agreed to give him the last of the water. As I poured the final drop into his bowl and watched his tail give a weak wag, I remembered the plastic soda bottleful of water Mrs. Shoemaker had said Max needed. I felt an unexpected surge of matureness. I was responsible for Max. I needed to find him more water. Immediately or sooner.

"Let's get going," I said. "If we need to, we can find our way back to this cactus with our rock trail. I think we should head down to that low spot there"—I pointed—"and look for the stream. If we can find the stream, we'll have water, but we'll also have a way back to the moms."

"How?" asked Marvin. This wasn't in his notebook, apparently.

In my mind's eye* I could see the map I'd drawn earlier in this notebook, which I'd left in the tent. "The main trail follows the stream, right? All we have to do is walk along the stream in the same direction that the water is flowing, and we'll be able to find the campsite and the moms."

"What about staying put?"

"If we don't find water, Max will die of dehydration." Even as I said it, I knew it was true. Like, actually true. My throat clenched.

"What if we cannot find the stream?"

I wasn't ready to consider that possibility. "We'll cross that bridge when we come to it."

I put on 1 of the random socks from my daypack, to replace the sock that was now full of prickers. I put the dirty underwear on my head, so my scalp wouldn't get any more sunburnt than it already was. And the 3 of us strode off toward what I hoped like heck was water and the way back to the moms.

I WOULD RAISE MY DETERMINED FIST HIGHER... BUT THIS SHIRT IS WAY TOO TIGHT.

My grandma, Goosy, always tells me to make a brain picture of what I want to happen. "Visualize your hopes and dreams," she says, "and they're more likely to become real." As we walked, I pictured heavy water bottles and Max drinking his fill and streams and rivers and mom hugs and the minivan and the air-conditioned car ride back to my house and my laptop and electricity and clean clothes and a shower—what?—and my luxurious life amid all of my family (even Timothy) and friends.

But then good ol' Marvin interrupted my musing.* "Look at this," he said. He was ahead of me a bit, and I hustled to catch up. He pointed at the ground. He'd just dropped a stone to mark our path, and the stone had landed in the middle of a shape on a muddy patch of ground.

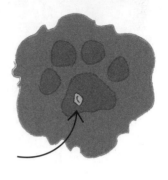

"Dude!" I said. "That's Max's paw print! We must have passed this way before! Maybe that means we're close to the stream!"

"I do not think it is a dog print," Marvin said, consulting his notebook. "It is wider, and I cannot see the claws in the impression. Also, Max is wearing booties. I believe it belongs to a mountain lion. It is a fresh track. That means the lion may be nearby. And the print is headed in the same direction we are."

And just like that, my lovely daydreams turned to visions way too bloody and morbid* to describe in a kid's sketchbook.

DOG, WOLF AND COYOTE TRACKS
☑ CLAW MARKS
☑ FRONT TOES ARE EVEN
☑ STAR BETWEEN PADS

CAT TRACKS
☑ NO CLAW MARKS
☑ SINGLE LEADING TOE
☑ "C" BETWEEN PADS

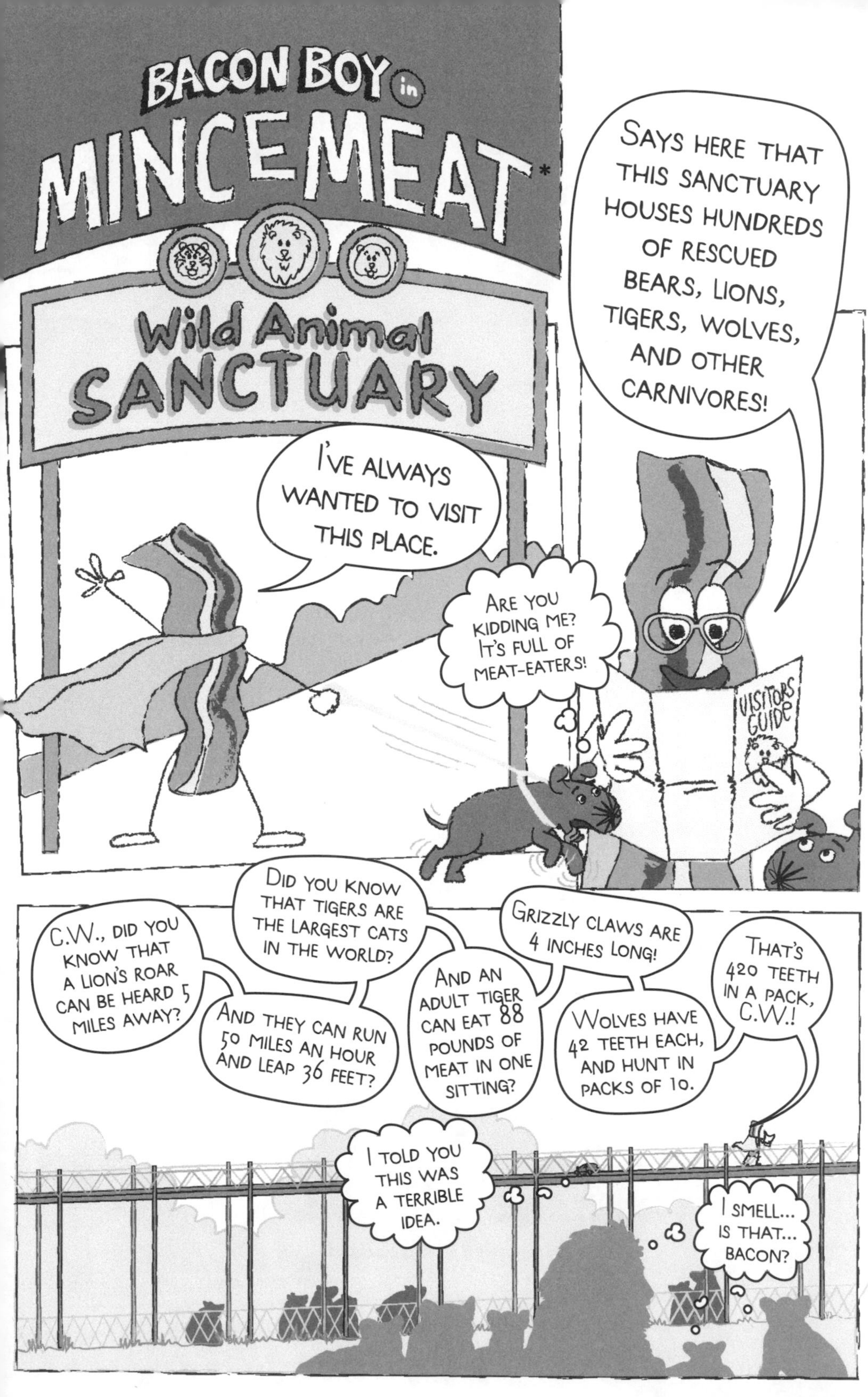
BACON BOY in
MINCEMEAT*
Wild Animal SANCTUARY
I'VE ALWAYS WANTED TO VISIT THIS PLACE.
SAYS HERE THAT THIS SANCTUARY HOUSES HUNDREDS OF RESCUED BEARS, LIONS, TIGERS, WOLVES, AND OTHER CARNIVORES!
ARE YOU KIDDING ME? IT'S FULL OF MEAT-EATERS!
VISITORS GUIDE
C.W., DID YOU KNOW THAT A LION'S ROAR CAN BE HEARD 5 MILES AWAY?
DID YOU KNOW THAT TIGERS ARE THE LARGEST CATS IN THE WORLD?
AND THEY CAN RUN 50 MILES AN HOUR AND LEAP 36 FEET?
AND AN ADULT TIGER CAN EAT 88 POUNDS OF MEAT IN ONE SITTING?
GRIZZLY CLAWS ARE 4 INCHES LONG!
WOLVES HAVE 42 TEETH EACH, AND HUNT IN PACKS OF 10.
THAT'S 420 TEETH IN A PACK, C.W.!
I TOLD YOU THIS WAS A TERRIBLE IDEA.
I SMELL... IS THAT... BACON?

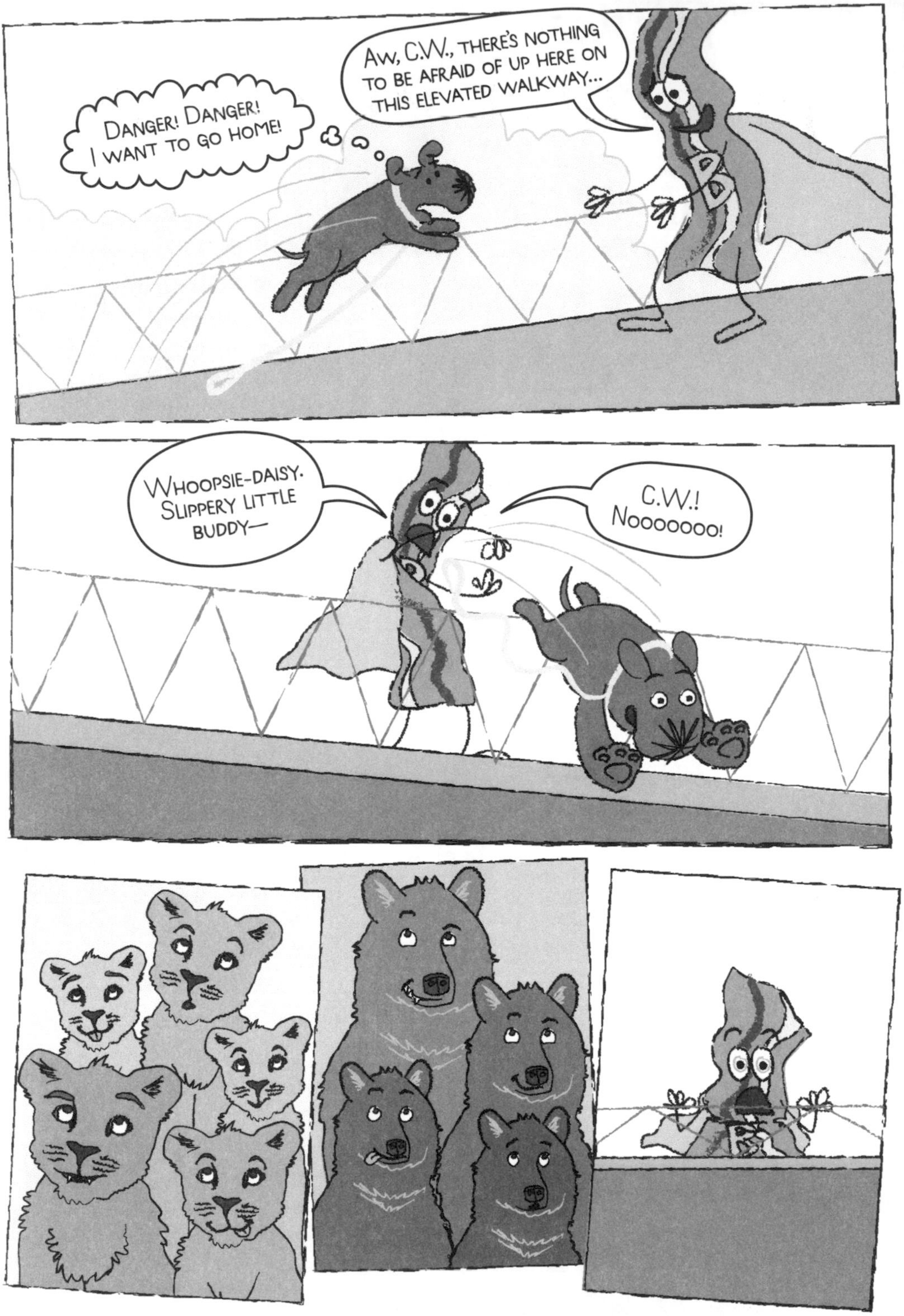
DANGER! DANGER! I WANT TO GO HOME!
AW, C.W., THERE'S NOTHING TO BE AFRAID OF UP HERE ON THIS ELEVATED WALKWAY...
WHOOPSIE-DAISY. SLIPPERY LITTLE BUDDY—
C.W.! NOOOOOOO!

TO BE CONTINUED...

JUST GIVE ME A SIGN

"I don't know what to do," I moaned. I was talking to myself, and to Marvin, and to Max, and to any ancestral wilderness gods that might be listening. "This is all my fault."

Max lay on his side, panting. Marvin patted me on the back, not hard and firm like a dad, but not soft and rubby like a mom, either. More mechanically,* like a window shutter banging in the wind.

I kept staring at the pawprint, like it would tell me what do if I just gawked at it long enough. Then I clapped my hands to my underweared head and looked up at the sky, like you do when you need a miracle. But instead, I saw a speck that became a black blob that became a bird flying toward us. It landed on the pawprint and peered up at us.

"*Pica hudsonia*," said Marvin. "The black-billed magpie."

"It's my mascot animal," I said. "And just like always, it's here to mock me. To remind me I'm a mooch. And a moron.*"

"You are not a moron," Marvin said.

The magpie began to hop. It bounced away from us, in roughly the same direction we'd been heading but more to the right. It kept hopping and hopping. Then it stopped and turned back to eyeball us.

"Weird," I said. "I think it wants us to follow it." In case of a mountain lion, I got out my slingshot, cocked a stone in its pouch, and single-filed behind the magpie. Max followed too. "Be ready with the bear spray," I directed Marvin, but when I glanced over, I saw that he was already holding the spray can out in front of him like a movie pistol.

The magpie took us down a hill and into a rocky canyon.

"This looks familiar," Marvin said.

Pretty soon the magpie hopped onto a brown rock. Only as I got closer I could see it wasn't a rock, it was the hat I'd lost in the flash flood. "Good bird!" I said, and I pulled the hat over my headerwear. "The stream's gotta be close!"

We rounded another corner, and there on a rock face were petroglyphs. The pictures showed stick-figure people and animals gathered along the edge of a skinny river. Some were predators, and some were prey, but it didn't matter, because all of them had come for the water.

"Dude," I said. "I could draw it better. But this is another sign!"

Max cocked his head then pulled me forward. And sure enough, there was the trickly stream. While he guzzled and gulped, Marvin and I worked together to pump water through the purifier and into our bottles. We drank and purified and filled again. The magpie dipped his beak quite a few times too. I know I said earlier that pillows are life, and they are, but man, water is lifer.

"OK," I said when we'd drunk our fill. "Now let's follow the stream to the moms."

The water was like gasoline in our tanks; it fueled us to keep going. We walked, and the magical magpie flew ahead of us, landing once in a while so we could catch up. The landscape got greener and the mosquitoes thicker.

We were out of the sheltering shade of the canyon now. The sun fried us like eggs, a thought that made me hungrier and also miss my dad, who's the breakfast-maker in my family. Not including the sun, the sky was a bright blue canvas. Except for those weird gray clouds over there, floating up from the top of that clump of trees...

"Hey!" I yelled. I stopped and pointed. "Those aren't clouds!"

"Correct," said Marvin. "They are smoke signals."

"They're smoke signals!" I shouted. "The moms must have started a giant, smokey campfire to signal us! We just have to walk toward the smoke! Wait a second...you knew that already? Why didn't you say something?"

"I just noticed it," Marvin said. "I also just noticed that." And he pointed to the top of a rock outcropping, ahead of us and to the right.

I knew I was hallucinating from hunger and exhaustion, but it looked like a cat. A cat sitting on its rear end and demurely licking a front paw.

THE HUMANS GO MARCHING 2 BY 2. HURRAH, HURRAH!

I chuckled to myself. "Must be a marmot* or something," I muttered. "Cats don't live in the wilderness. I'll snap an epic pic and look at it later, after I've found all my marbles.*" I pulled my phone from my pocket, but the battery was dead.

"GO AWAY!" Marvin's shout startled me. I swiveled my head and saw that he wasn't just bellowing, he was jumping up and down and waving his arms. "GO AWAY! GO AWAY!"

I looked back at the marmot, who was ambling in our direction, its long, black-tipped tail flowing behind.

The part of my brain that didn't want to believe it was a mountain lion began to face the facts: <u>of course it was a mountain lion!!!</u>

"IT'S A MOUNTAIN LION!" I screamed. "WE HAVE TO CLUMP TOGETHER AND MAKE OURSELVES LOOK BIG AND WAVE OUR ARMS!" I flung my limbs every which way. Max joined in with his most murderous* barks.

Added to Marvin's shouts and Max's barks, my freak-out seemed to make the mountain lion pause. He stopped about 10 minivan-lengths away. But I thought he had a hungry look in his eyes. I knew how he felt. How many days had it been since either one of us had had fresh meat?

Then I remembered the slingshot. I handed Marvin Max's leash and pulled a stone from my pocket. I launched it lionward. I missed! I zinged another one. It hit the ground in front of him then bounced up and plinked him in his furry chest. He tipped his head to the side and opened his tooth-filled mouth. Out came a hiss followed by a deep, rumbly growl. He stepped toward us.

"WHEN HE IS 30 FEET AWAY, I WILL SPRAY THE BEAR SPRAY!" Marvin shouted.

"OK!" I yelled, because that's all we did now—yell. "BUT HOW CAN YOU TELL WHERE 30 FEET IS?!"

S-S-S-ORRY! I G-G-G-UESS I F-F-F-ORGOT TO P-P-P-ACK MY T-T-T-APE MEASURE...!

In the commotion, an annoying cheep sound to my left made me turn my head. The magpie! I'd forgotten about him too. He was strutting and pecking at the ground. I looked closer and saw that he was kind of herding something in my direction. Gah! A mouse! A scurrying little devil creature! Fleeing the magpie, the mouse ran toward me, and fleeing the mouse, I ran...

...toward the mountain lion. "**AHHH!**" I yelled like a berzerk maniac.* "**AHHHHHHHHHH!!!**"

The next thing I knew the world was dark and my head throbbed. Was my noggin inside of the lion's mouth? Was I being eaten alive?

Then I felt Max's familiar doggy tongue on my face and Marvin's wiry arms helping me sit up and handing me water to drink.

"You are OK," he said. "You tripped and fell splat on your face."

"What happened to the mm..." I was going to say "mouse" but caught myself and instead said "...mountain lion?" I spit out a pebble, but when I saw it bloody white on the ground, I realized it was a chunk of tooth.

"The mountain lion ran away. He was afraid of you."

"Darn right he was." I got to my feet, dusted myself off, and immediately set to hiking again. Marvin and Max and I continued downstream, toward the smoke clouds. I whistled merrily, though I had to adjust my whistling technique to accommodate the the new gap between my front teeth. I kept my eyes peeled, but I didn't see the mountain lion or the mouse or the magpie again.

Tired as we were, Marvin went back to zig-zagging back and forth and jumping on and off rocks. We switched shirts, because he wanted his back. If you have to be lost in a desolate, dangerous wilderness, turns out Marvin Shoemaker is a pretty good outdoorsperson to be lost with, all things considered.

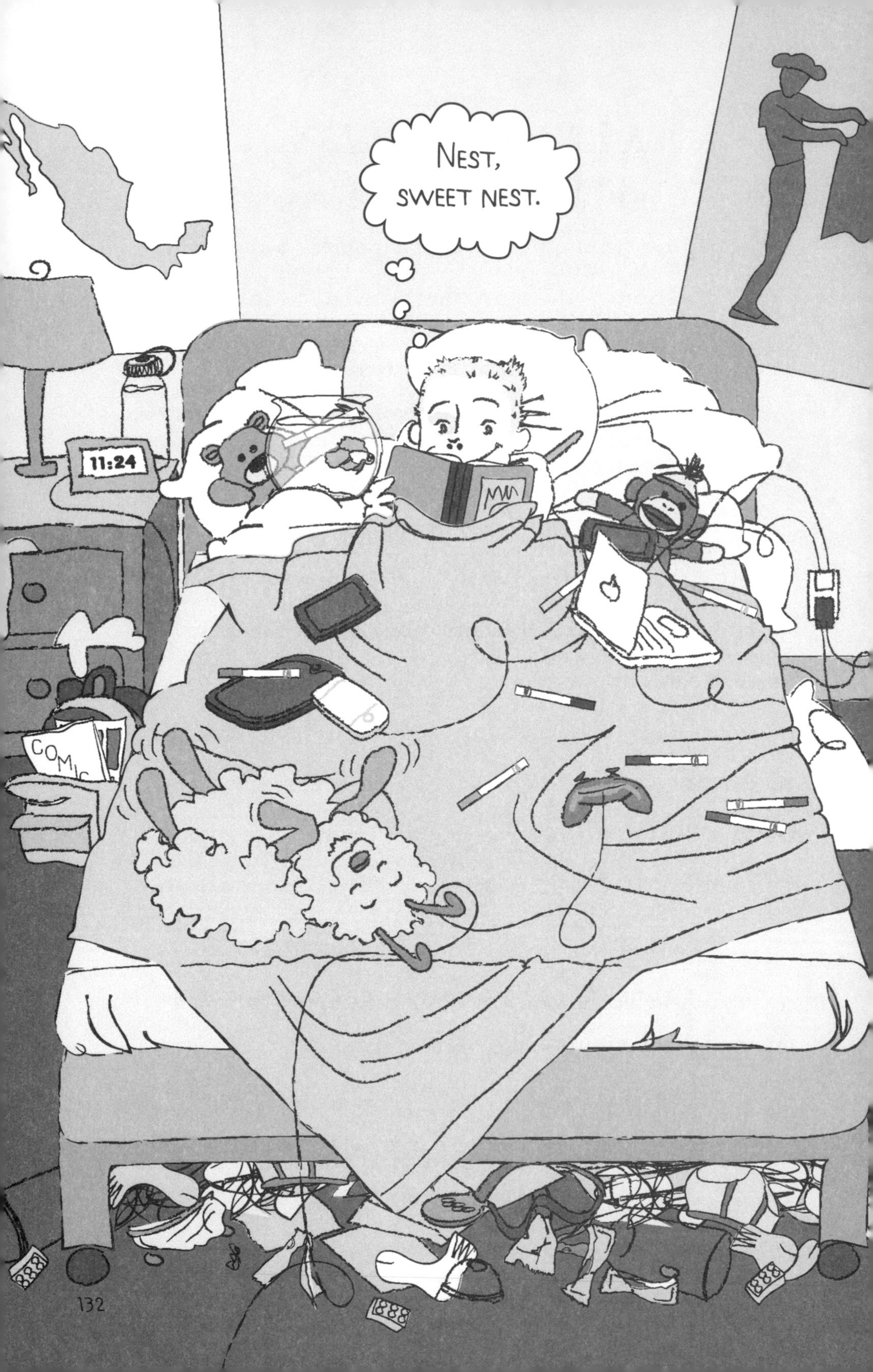
NEST,
SWEET NEST.
11:24
COMIC

ALDO'S WELL
IN THE END

I know I said that after water, pillows are life, but it's actually beds that are life. I'm in mine now, in my indoor bedroom in my awesome house, with Max and my betta fish, Bogus, sketchbooking the final chapters of this harrowing true story.

Marvin and I did make it back to camp. We followed the stream and the smoke signals, and there it was. If you've ever had a mother worry about you, you can imagine the scene when we stumbled into the clearing with the belching smoke and the waiting moms. Never in my life have I participated in so much hugging and crying and exclaiming. It was an awfully moist reunion.

My mom kissed me all over my sweaty, dirty, sunburnt face. In her motherly frenzy, she even got my nose holes, just like that mama elk. Gross. "Oh, Aldo!" she sobbed, because crying _is_ part of being mature, I realized. "I'm sorry I made it sound like you should grow up faster. I love you just the way you are!"

"It's OK," I said with my mouth mooshed into her shoulder. Her hug was the opposite of getting lost. I pulled away and looked her in the face. "But I did take care of myself. I found food. And water. Actually, Marvin and me, we took care of each other. And Max."

Mrs. Shoemaker tended to Max, who needed food and more water and a bandage for one of his paws, where the bootie had torn. My mom cooked the remaining blue-packet meals for me and Marvin. While we ate and rested, we told the moms everything that happened on our adventure, including the mountain lion part. The moms' mouths were so agape I wondered if Mexican Spotted Owls might nest in them.

"Aldo chased the mountain lion away," Marvin said. "That was not on the list. But it saved us. I will add it to the list."

I shrugged. I didn't mention the mouse. That'll remain a little secret between the magpie and me.

We camped in the same spot that night. The next morning, we hiked back to the minivan. Upholstery! Air conditioning! Electronics! We drove to Bears Ears National Monument for an epic pic...

DOG EARS

BEARS EARS

BUNNY EARS

DIRTY EARS

...then headed home. On the way, we stopped in Moab for a supersize lunch at McDonald's. And guess who we saw there? Miles! That kid who babysat Max at Mesa Verde! Only this time he somehow seemed littler. Weird.

When we got to Fort Collins, we dropped off Marvin and Mrs. Shoemaker at their house, which isn't too far away from mine. Mom and I helped them unload. While the moms jabbered and Max rolled around in the grass, Marvin and I stood there. Well, he didn't so much stand as fidget. Then he unzipped his daypack.

"Here," he said. He handed me the cave skull.

"It's yours," I said, although now that we were back in civilization, it did seem like a way-cool keepsake.

"I am giving it to you," he said.

I unzipped my daypack and handed him the slingshot. "Here," I said.

Marvin extended his left hand. "Shake," he said.

"No, you shake with <u>this</u> hand," I said, putting out my right hand.

"Boy Scouts shake left," he said.

So I grabbed Marvin's left hand with my left hand, and we shook.

"All's well that ends well," I said.

"Aldo is well in the end," he said.

Both of us were right.

BACON BOY in "MISSED MEAT"

At the end of our last episode, Bacon Boy and his faithful dog, C.W., were visiting the Wild Animal Sanctuary when C.W. slipped from the overhead viewing walkway and was seen falling to the hungry lions and bears waiting below...

HELP! HELP! HEEELLLPPP!!!

Mea culpa,* C.W.! I'll save you!

Hey dog. There's a fence down here, ya know...

Plus they feed us plenty of raw meat...

Yeah, we're not really even that hungry...

Oh.

We were just watching to see if cocktail weenies really do land on all fours.

COWABUNGA!

SPLAT

Just because you wear a cape doesn't mean you can fly, my friend. Now let's get outta here before they change their minds!

They seemed like good guys... but I'm trying to eat more healthy.

You know what snack is good AND good for you?

A nice, tender MOUSE!

MALAPROPISMS: A MINI-LESSON

After I finished filling up this M sketchbook, I showed it to Mr. Mot, like I always do. First he said it was meaningful. Whatever. Then he told me it contains "malapropisms," which are when you accidentally use the wrong word in place of a right word that sounds similar. For an example, if my pillow had gotten too close to the campfire and burst into flames (gah!), I might have freaked out and yelled, "Get the fire distinguisher!" when what I really meant was "fire extinguisher."

There are also things called "mondegreens," which are kinda like malapropisms, except they're when you misunderstand or mishear something then you repeat it incorrectly. So the next time you hear a kid say something not-quite-right during a song or the Pledge of Allegiance (like "...and to the Republic, for witches stand..."), you'll know that's a mondegreen.

Mr. Mot pointed out a bunch of malapropisms in Mooch. Marvin's a malapropism master, so I think they should be called "Marvinisms."

"MARVINISM"	ACTUAL SAYING
P. 16 THE EARLY WORM GETS TO SQUIRM.	P. 16 THE EARLY BIRD GETS THE WORM.
P. 37 DOT THE FLIES AND CROSS THE BEES.	P. 37 DOT THE I'S AND CROSS THE T'S.
P. 72 A CLIMB AT 9 SAVES A STITCH OF TIME.	P. 72 A STITCH IN TIME SAVES 9.
P. 87 ALDO'S WELL IN THE END.	P. 87 ALL'S WELL THAT ENDS WELL.

"MARVINISM"	ACTUAL SAYING
P. 91 LIKE A SQUARE AT THE FAIR.	P. 91 FAIR AND SQUARE.
P. 99 MIND YOUR OWN WILDERNESS. (I DID NOT SAY THIS ONE!)	P. 99 MIND YOUR OWN BUSINESS. (I KNOW. I DID.)
P. 130 SPLAT ON YOUR FACE.	P. 130 FLAT ON YOUR FACE.
P. 137 MISSED MEAT.	P. 137 MINCEMEAT.

"M" GALLERY

Mr. Mot used to be an English teacher. He's a word nerd, and he likes to help me use awesome words in my sketchbooks. I mark the best words with one of these:* (it's called an asterisk). When you see an * you'll know you can look here, in the Gallery, to see what the word means. If you don't know how to say some of the words, just ask Mr. Mot. Or someone you know who's like Mr. Mot. Or go to aldozelnick.com, and we'll say them for you.

mad about you (pg. 3): When someone loves you so much they can hardly stand it.

mad skills (pg. 18): so good at something you should make You-Tube videos of yourself doing it

maddening (pg. 112): Gah!-level irritating

madwoman (pg. 38): crazy-weird mom-type

maelstrom (pg. 83): a stormy rush

magenta (pg. 117): purply-red

magnanimous (pg. 78): generous

magnetic (pg. 68): something that draws people to it, like my magnificent personality

magnificent (pg. 13): really wonderful

majesty (pg. 39): impressive beauty

malarkey (pg. 98): blah-blah-blah nonsense

malevolent (pg. 77): mean and evil

malnourished (pg. 98): weak from not being fed enough for days

mammalian (pg. 39): for mammals, which are animals that lay babies instead of eggs

mammoth (NOT ACTUAL SIZE) (pg. 29): behemoth-big; ginormous

manageable (pg. 32): doable like it's no big deal

maniac (pg. 130): wild and loud person

manlier (pg. 12): taking another step away from boyness and toward full-grown manness

manna (pg. 77): magical stuff that falls from the sky to save you

manual labor (pg. 57): work you have to do with your hands and muscles

manured (pg. 59): animal-pooped

marbles, lose your (pg. 127): when you're thinking crazy

Marine (pg. 13): tough military guy

141

marmot (pg. 127): a giant squirrel that lives in the mountains. I kid you not.

marveling (pg. 14): gazing at with wonder

mascot (pg. 28): an animal that's supposed to represent you or bring you luck

masquerade (pg. 51): a pretend show

mass (pg. 84): the size and shape and weight of you

mastery (pg. 39): getting to be master-level good at something

masticating (pg. 88): chewing

maternal units (pg. 73): mothers

matters into my own hands, take (pg. 99): take charge of something yourself

matter-of-fact (pg. 65): like it's obvious and no big deal

matter of life and death (pg. 27): something that might kill you if you do it wrong

mature (pg. 12): independent and grown-up-like. Ugh! Being a kid is way better.

mauled (pg. 9): wounded by a fierce animal

mayhem (pg. 82): messy trouble

mea culpa (pg. 137): my bad

meager (pg. 108): less than what is needed

meander (pg. 101): walk in a twisty, random way

measly (pg. 42): same as meager, basically

measuredly (pg. 90): carefully and calmly

mechanically (pg. 123): like a machine would

medium-rare (pg. 14): the perfect, pink-inside doneness of red-blooded meats

meek (pg. 78): shy and gentle

meh (pg. 16): OK-but-not-that-special

melancholy (pg. 113): sad and sad and sad

melee (pg. 82): a chaotic disruption; brouhaha

mellowly (pg. 60): calmly and chillaxedly

meltdowns (pg. 13): tantrums or freak-outs

memorable (pg. 3): so cool you can't forget it

menacing (pg. 51): snarly-mean-looking-and-sounding

mendacious (pg. 98): lying

menfolk (pg. 14): the guys

menial (pg. 56): petty, boring, and annoyingly workish

merciless (pg. 59): keeps being mean to you even when it's easy to see you're struggling

merrymaking (pg. 70): pure fun, with no physical or emotional torture mixed in

Mesa Verde National Park (pg. 7): a place in the lower-left corner of my state (Colorado) where you can see major ruins and learn about how the Ancestral Puebloans lived

method to your madness (pg. 3): knowing what you're doing even though it looks like you don't

midday (pg. 77): about halfway through the light part of the day. Lunchtime.

Middle East (pg. 8): the sandy part of the globe where Europe and Asia and Africa come together and 411 million people live there

middle of nowhere (pg. 111): a place where hardly anyone lives and hardly anything happens except nature

middle school (pg. 12): First comes elementary then middle, then high. So... how come elementary isn't called "low school"?

midway (pg. 7): about halfway

miffed (pg. 75): mad

millisecond (pg. 8): 1 one-thousandth of a second

milquetoast (pg. 52): timid

mimicked (pg. 74): copied the sounds or motions of something

minced (pg. 69): walked delicately, with short, fast steps

mincemeat (pg. 121): completely destroyed or annihilated, like chewed-up meat

mind's eye, in my (pg. 118): in an epic pic in my imagination

miniscule (pg. 61): tiny; diminutive; miniature; Lilliputian

minister (pg. 75): take care of

mirage (pg. 115): good stuff your mind imagines

miscreant (pg. 59): bad evildoer

misery (pg. 38): when you hurt inside and out, usually for a while

mite (pg. 56): an itty-bit

moan (pg. 71): make pitiful, needy noises

mocked (pg. 108): enjoyed making me feel foolish

moderating (pg. 101): making something that's large get smaller

modicum (pgs. 3 and 114): a little bit

moist (pg. 68): kinda wet; damp

moisture (pg. 61): liquids (usually water) that make things moist

moldering (pg. 112): decaying and falling apart

molecule (pg. 113): The cells in your body are made of molecules, which are made of atoms.

mollified (pg. 103): calmed down

mondo (pg. 33): humongous

monoliths (pg. 71): big towers of rock sticking up into the sky

monologue (pg. 97): when 1 person hogs the conversation for a while with a long solo speech

mooches (pg. 9): A mooch is someone who uses/borrows/takes other people's stuff instead of being responsible for his own. Yeahhh...

moonstruck (pg. 66): acting crazy because of the full moon (or, heh, possibly getting struck by the sight of someone mooning you)

mooshed (pgs. 75 and 134): flattened in a blobby, uneven way

morbid (pg. 120): icky and disturbing and macabre

morning person (pg. 21): a weirdo who likes to get up early

moron (pg. 123): uber-dumb person

morsel (pg. 8): tiny bit

mortal (pg. 112): something alive that eventually dies

mortal danger (pg. 50): danger that could kill you

mosied (pg. 25): moved ahead in a slow and aimless way

motherliness (pg. 98): that way moms are when they're worried about you

motley (pg. 11): random and kinda lame

mountain man (pg. 100): a guy who's a super-great outdoorsperson, especially in mountainy wilderness

mournfully (pg. 63): with noticeable sadness

mouth-breathing (pg. 95): inhaling and exhaling through your open mouth instead of your nose holes like you're supposed to!

mouthwatering (pg. 78): so yummy your mouth starts making lots of spit

muddled (pg. 80): mixed-up

muffled (pg. 73): when something gets in a sound's way

muffuletta (pg. 51): a sandwich with chopped olives, cheese, and <u>4 kinds</u> of Italian pork meats!

> MF-MF-MF

mule deer (pg. 15): the kind of deer that live where I do

mulish (pg. 80): sounding kinda donkey-like

mumbo-jumbo (pg. 41): malarkey

munchkin (pg. 3): a small human

munchies (pg. 8): snacky-mild hungriness

munificently (pg. 3): with generous helpfulness

murder, bloody (pg. 8): with great alarm, like you were in mortal danger*

murderous (pg. 128): mean and scary

musing (pg. 119): nice thoughts

mustered (pgs. 25 and 69): gathered together

mutilated (pg. 77): cut up and broken

mutiny (pg. 25): get mad and tell the leader you're not doing what she says anymore

muttered (pg. 21): said in a mumbly and quiet way

myriad (pg. 115): lots of

MANTI-LA SAL NATIONAL FOREST, UTAH

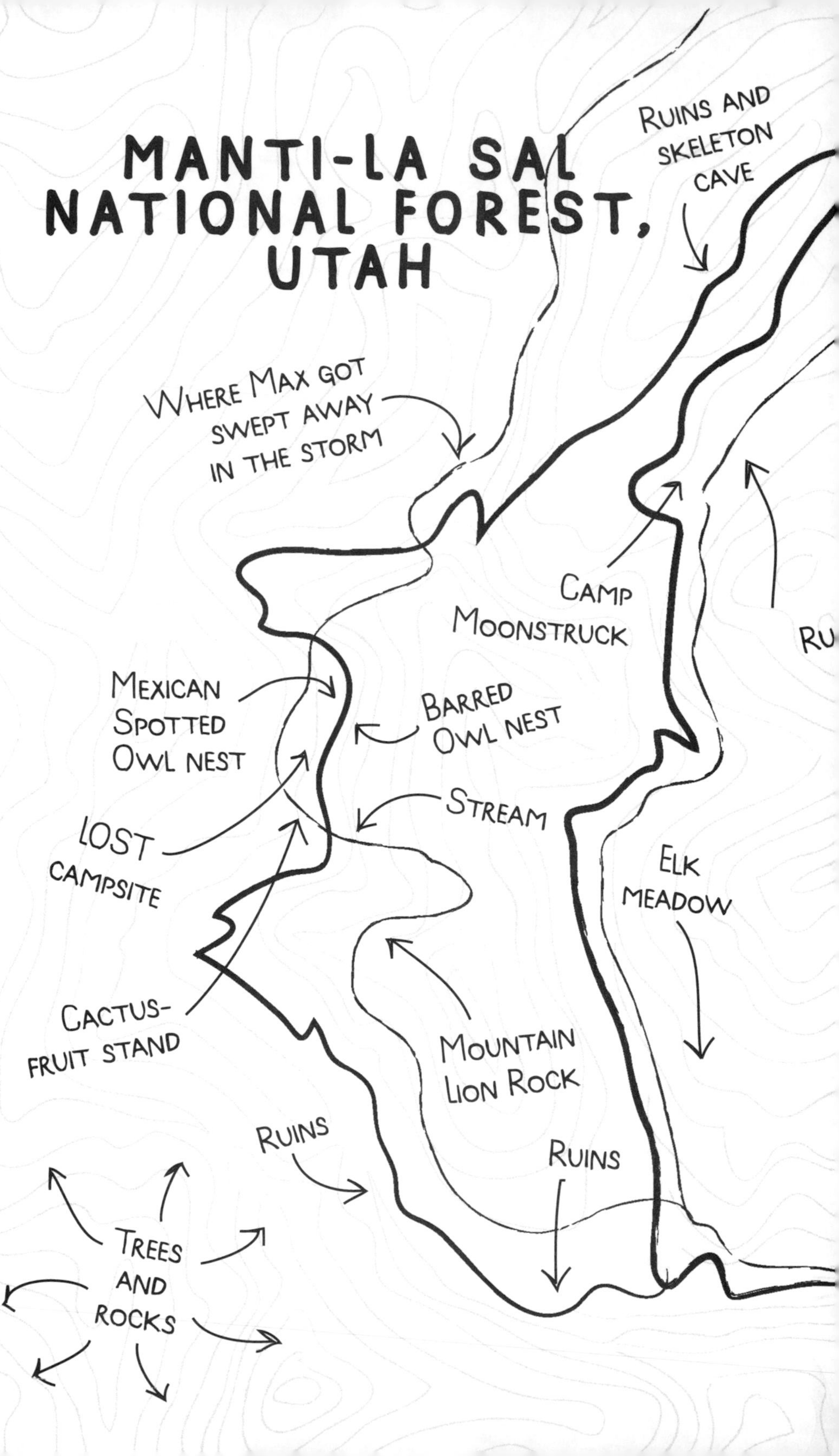
Ruins and skeleton cave
Where Max got swept away in the storm
Camp Moonstruck
Ru
Mexican Spotted Owl nest
Barred Owl nest
Stream
Lost campsite
Elk meadow
Cactus-fruit stand
Mountain Lion Rock
Ruins
Ruins
Trees and rocks

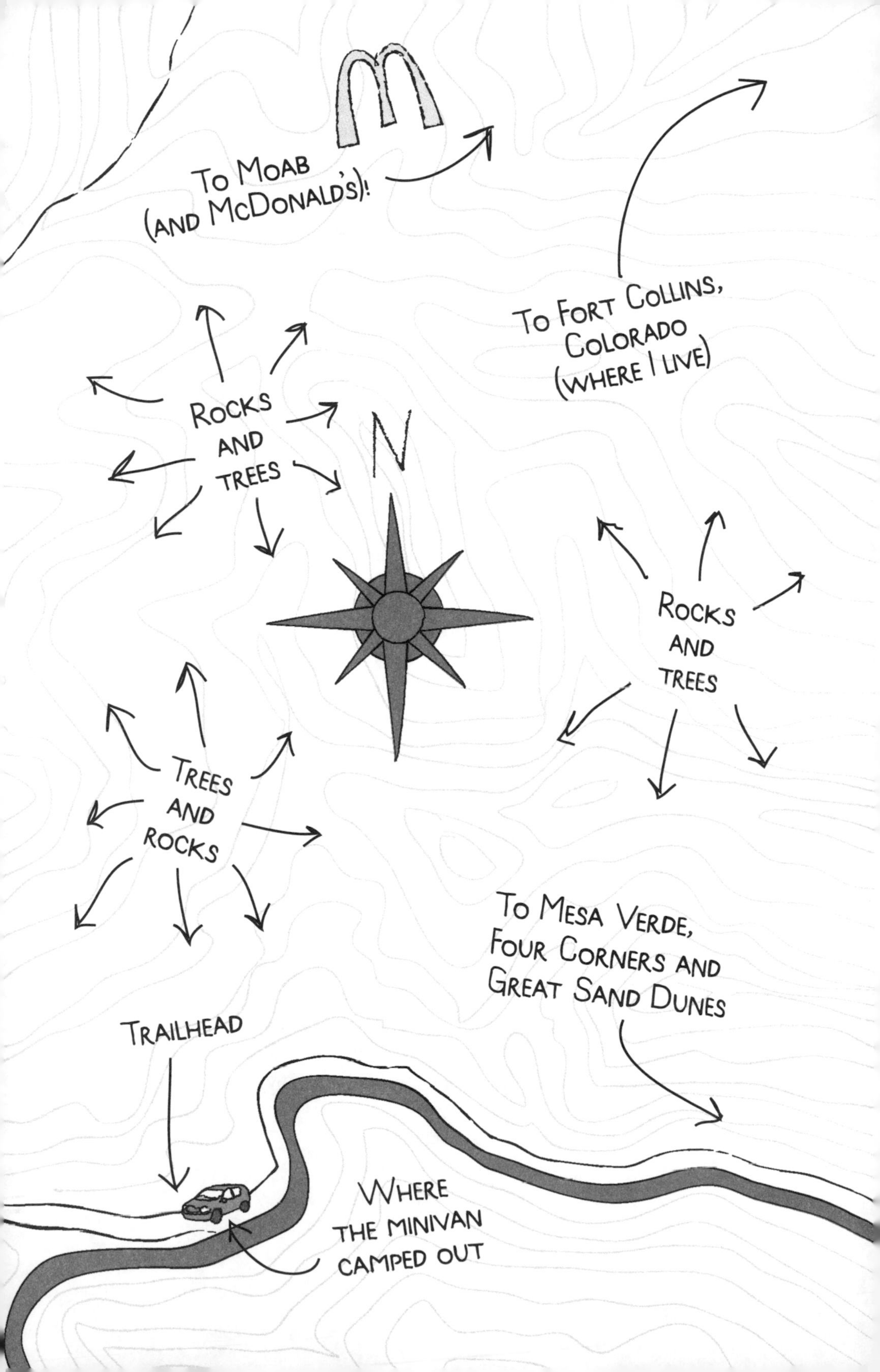
To Moab (and McDonald's)!
To Fort Collins, Colorado (where I live)
Rocks and trees
N
Rocks and trees
Trees and rocks
To Mesa Verde, Four Corners and Great Sand Dunes
Trailhead
Where the minivan camped out

award-winning

ABOUT THE ALDO ZELNICK COMIC NOVEL SERIES

The Aldo Zelnick comic novels are an alphabetical series for middle-grade readers aged 7-13. Rabid and reluctant readers alike enjoy the intelligent humor and drawings as well as the action-packed stories. They've been called vitamin-fortified *Wimpy Kids*.

Part comic romps, part mysteries, and part sesquipedalian-fests

(ask Mr. Mot), they're beloved by parents, teachers, and librarians as much as kids.

Artsy-Fartsy introduces ten-year-old Aldo, the star and narrator of the entire series, who lives with his family in Colorado. He's not athletic like his older brother, he's not a rock hound like his best friend, but he does like bacon. And when his artist grandmother, Goosy, gives him a sketchbook to "record all his artsy-fartsy

ideas" during summer vacation, it turns out Aldo is a pretty good cartoonist.

In addition to an engaging cartoon story, each book in the series includes an illustrated glossary of fun and challenging words used throughout the book, such as *absurd*, *abominable*, and *audacious* in *Artsy-Fartsy* and *brazen*, *behemoth*, and *boisterous* in *Bogus*.

BAILIWICK PRESS

www.bailiwickpress.com | www.aldozelnick.com

ALSO IN THE ALDO ZELNICK COMIC NOVEL SERIES

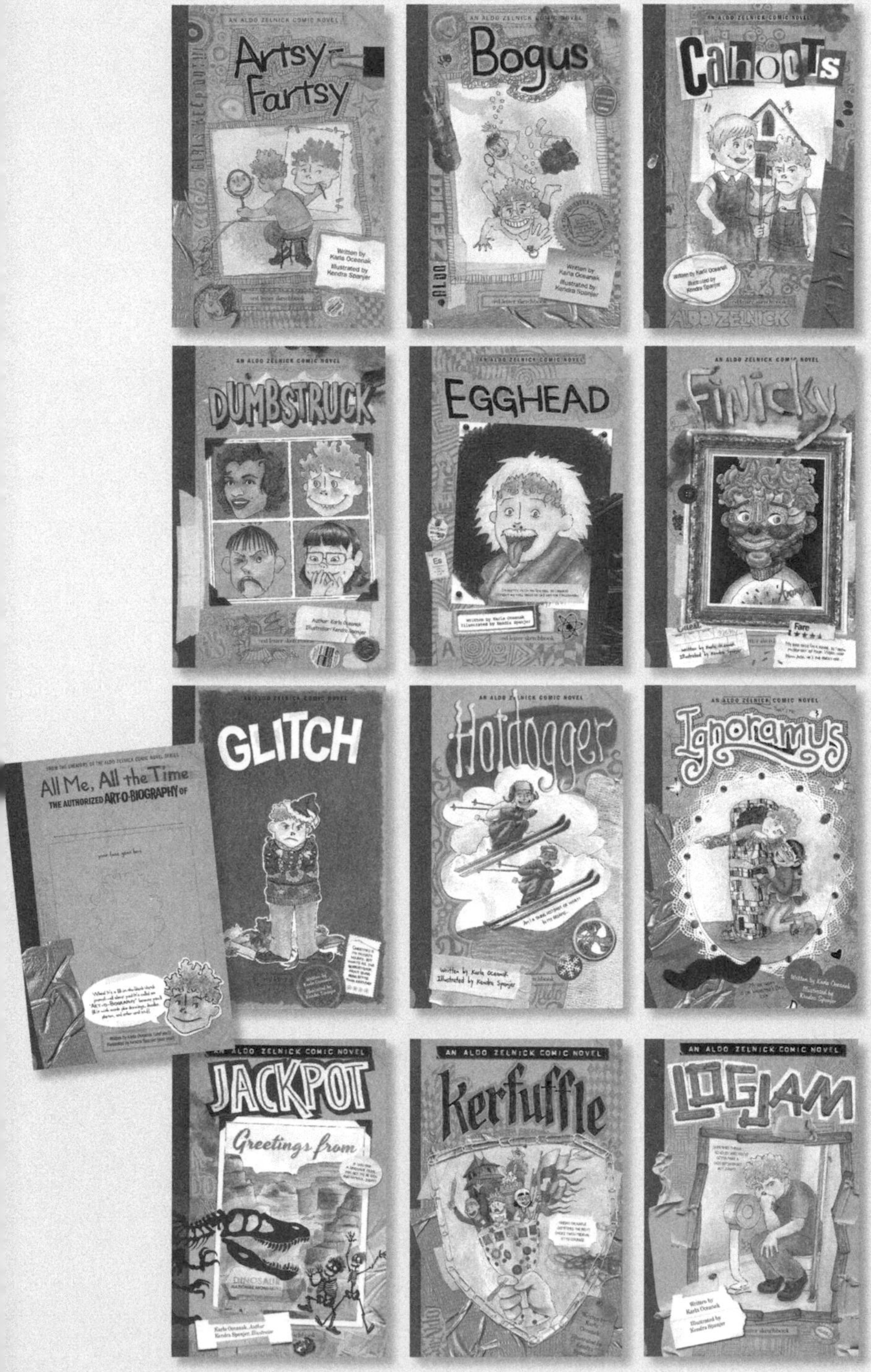
Artsy-Fartsy
Bogus
Cahoots
Dumbstruck
Egghead
Finicky
All Me, All the Time
THE AUTHORIZED ART-O-BIOGRAPHY OF
Glitch
Hotdogger
Ignoramus
Jackpot
Kerfuffle
Logjam

ALSO AVAILABLE IN SOFTCOVER!

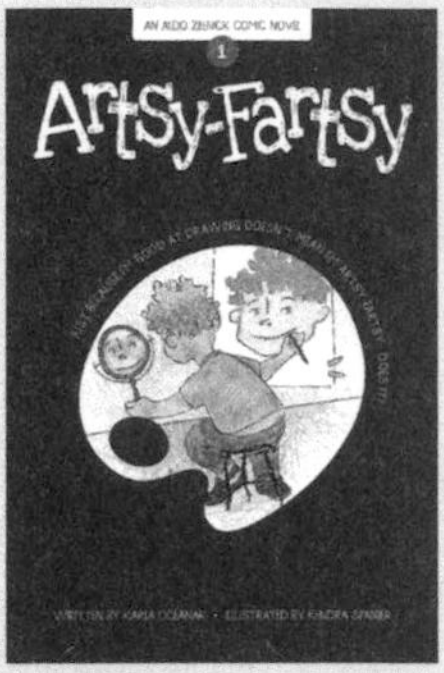
AN ALDO ZELNICK COMIC NOVEL
1
Artsy-Fartsy

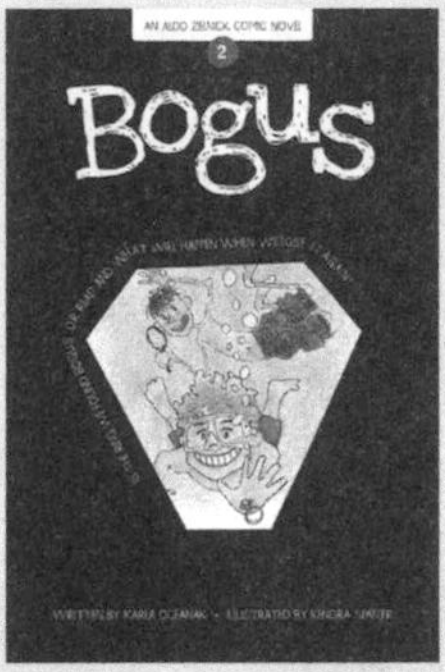
AN ALDO ZELNICK COMIC NOVEL
2
Bogus

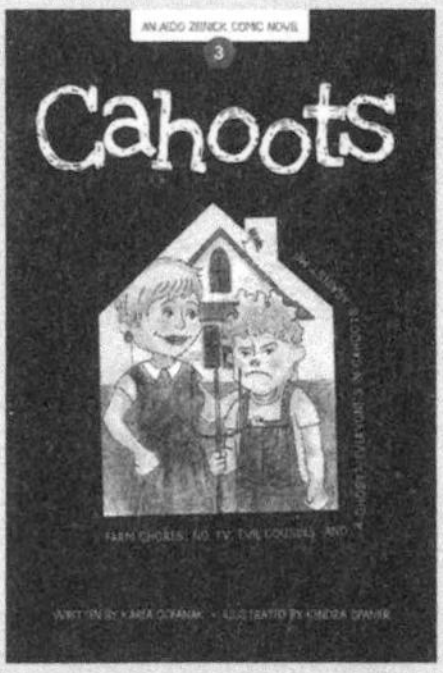
AN ALDO ZELNICK COMIC NOVEL
3
Cahoots

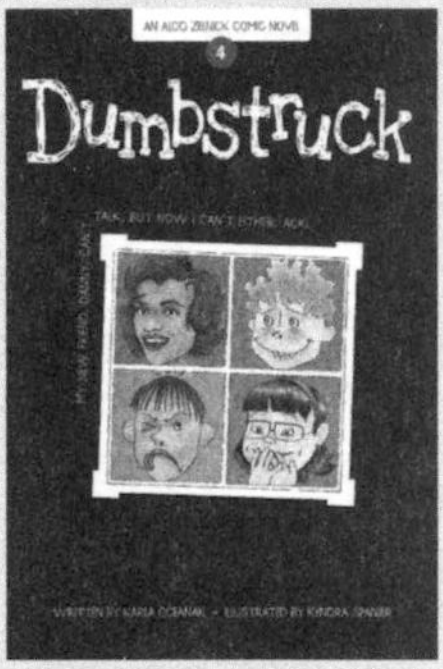
AN ALDO ZELNICK COMIC NOVEL
4
Dumbstruck

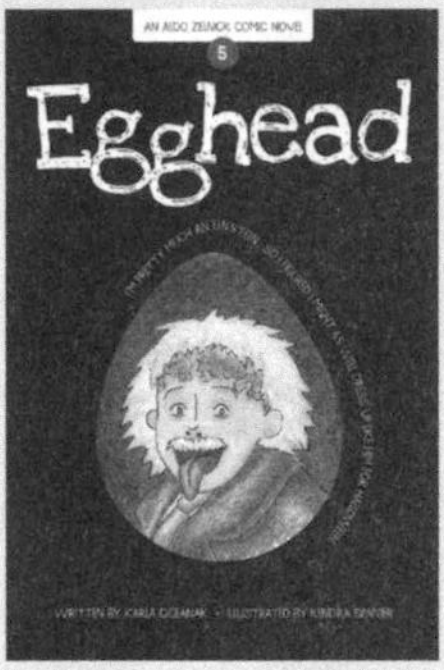
AN ALDO ZELNICK COMIC NOVEL
5
Egghead

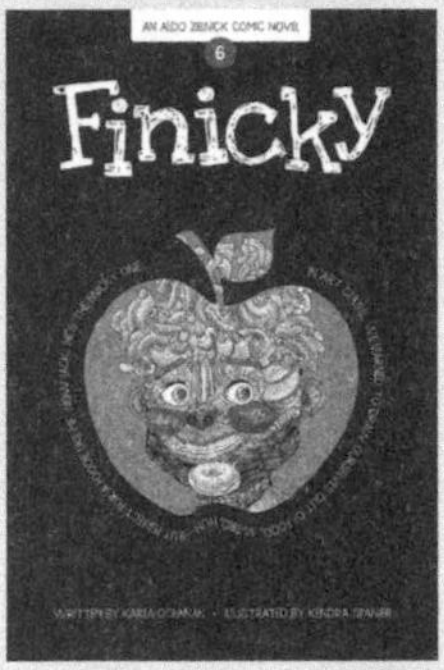
AN ALDO ZELNICK COMIC NOVEL
6
Finicky

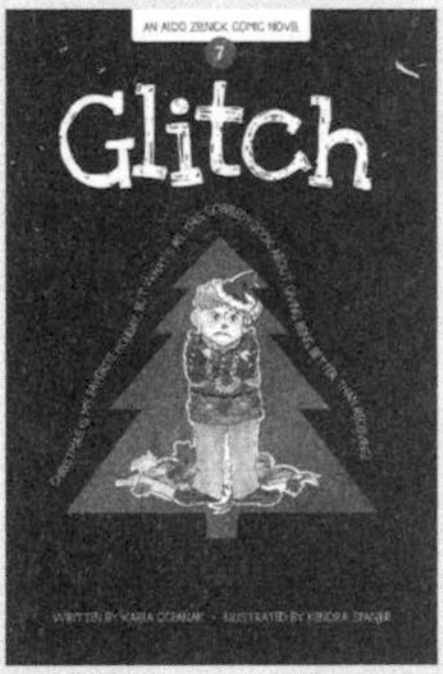
AN ALDO ZELNICK COMIC NOVEL
7
Glitch

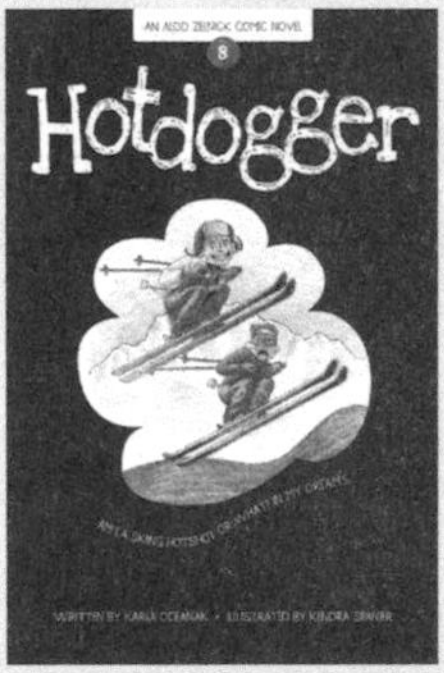
AN ALDO ZELNICK COMIC NOVEL
8
Hotdogger

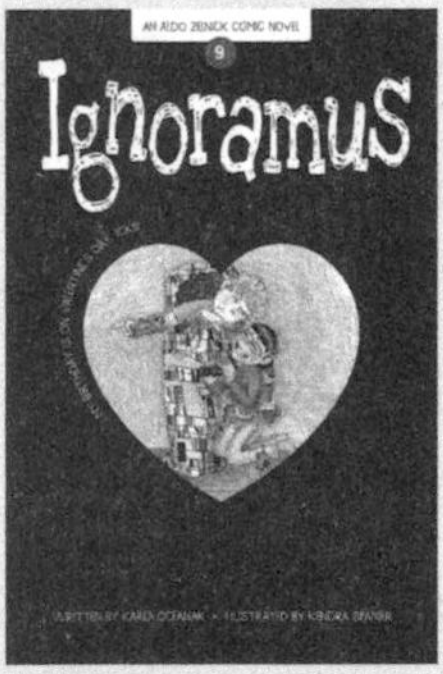
AN ALDO ZELNICK COMIC NOVEL
9
Ignoramus

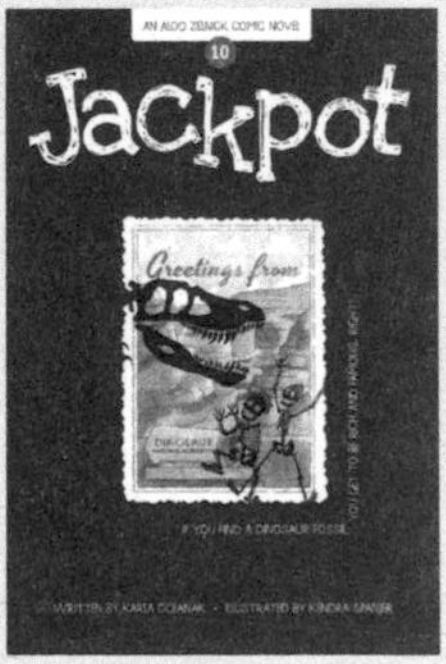
AN ALDO ZELNICK COMIC NOVEL
10
Jackpot
Greetings from

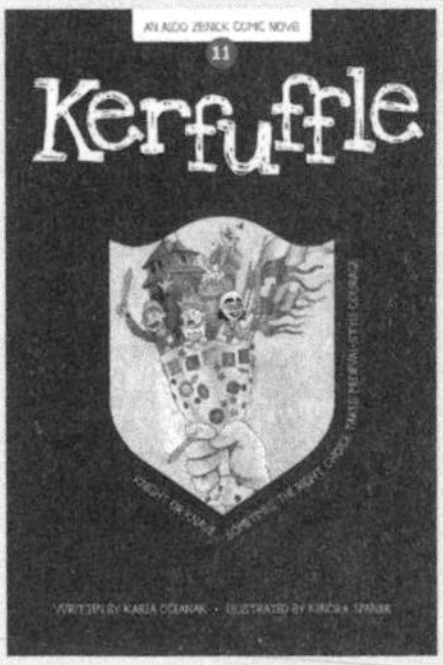
AN ALDO ZELNICK COMIC NOVEL
11
Kerfuffle

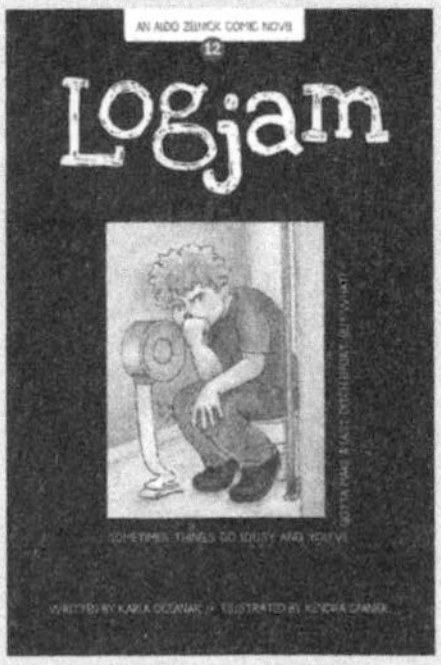
AN ALDO ZELNICK COMIC NOVEL
12
Logjam

THE ALDO ZELNICK FAN CLUB
IS FOR READERS OF ANY AGE WHO
LOVE THE BOOK SERIES AND
WANT THE INSIDE SCOOP ON
ALL THINGS ZELNICKIAN.

GO TO WWW.ALDOZELNICK.COM
AND CLICK ON THIS FLAG-THINGY!

SIGN UP TO RECEIVE:

- sneak preview chapters from the next book.
- an early look at coming book titles, covers, and more.
- opportunities to vote on new character names and other stuff.
- discounts on the books and merchandise.
- a card from Aldo on your birthday (for kids)!

The Aldo Zelnick fan club is free and easy.
If you're under 13, ask your mom or dad to sign you up!

WHAT READERS ARE SAYING:

(kid comments are in Aldo's handwriting)

"It was the funniest book I have ever read. The illustrations are hilarious. It is better than *Diary of a Wimpy Kid.*"

— Tavis

"The Aldo Zelnick books keep getting better and better."

— Mary Lee Hahn, teacher and readingyear.blogspot.com blogger

"You will laugh out loud—I guarantee it. The books are THAT funny."

— Becky Bilby, inthepages.blogspot.com

"I've been waiting for a series to come along that could knock Wimpy Kid off its pedestal as the most popular series in my library. Well, this may be it: the Aldo Zelnick Comic Novels. Save room on your shelves for 26 volumes!"

— Donna Dannenmiller, elementary librarian

"Aldo is pretty awesome in my book."

— Dr. Sharon Pajka, English professor, Gallaudet University

"The other night I caught my 8-year-old twins giggling on the living room couch as they took turns reading *Artsy-Fartsy* aloud to each other. Then one morning I found it on their nightstand with a headlamp resting on the cover from the previous night's under-cover reading. That's a true badge of honor in this house. You hit this one out of the park."

— Becky Jensen

"As a teacher of 20 years I have never come across a book that has engaged readers so intensely so quickly. The boys in my reading group devoured the series and were sad when they finished the most recent one."
— Cheryl Weber, Director of Educational Support,
Indian Community School

"One of the most remarkable things about these books is the voice of Aldo, which rings true from every page. The hilarious drawings enhance the text with jokes and visual humor that make Aldo's personality pop."
— Rebecca McGregor, Picture Literacy

"THE BOOK WAS VERY HILARIOUS. IT MADE US LAUGH OUT LOUD. YOU HAVE THE BEST CHARACTERS EVER!"
— Sebastian

"We recommend A is for Aldo! Hilarious stories, goofy drawings, and even sneaky new vocabulary words. If you are an admirer of *Diary of a Wimpy Kid*, you'll adore Aldo Zelnick."
— Oak Park Public Library

"I LOVE the Aldo Zelnick books so much that I want to read them for the rest of my life!"
— Gregory, age 9

"This terrific series will be enjoyed by all readers and constantly in demand. Highly recommended."
— South Sound Book Review Council of Washington libraries

"This is a fun series that my students adore."
— Katherine Sokolowski, 5th grade teacher

"Every library that serves Wimpy Kid fans (which, honestly, is every library, period) should have the Aldo Zelnick series on its shelves."

— Katie Ahearn, children's librarian, Washington DC

"Aldo is an endearing narrator. His deadpan sense of humor is enjoyable even for adults. Each book is a fast-paced, light read, perfect for the kid looking for a transition from comics to chapter books."

— Sarah, children's buyer, Left Bank Books

"When I am reading an Aldo Zelnick book in RTI, I don't want to go back to my classroom. Somehow I want to keep reading...and I don't like reading."

— an elementary student

"I am completely charmed by this series. The drawings and text have the quality of simultaneously being appealing to children and also amusing for adults. A big strength here is in the development of the characters. This is wonderful, since this is going to be an A to Z series and we'll have plenty of time to get to know them better. These are individuals with staying power. With the sketchbook comes a wonderful, not-overstated message of allowing Aldo to be himself and follow his creativity. Bravo!"

— Jean Hanson

"...a must for your elementary school reader."

— Christy, Reader's Cove bookstore

"In the wake of Wimpy Kid and Amelia's Notebooks comes Aldo Zelnick. Oceanak has created a funny and lively hero. The illustrations add to the humor."

— *Library Media Connection*

ACKNOWLEDGMENTS

"Be a sadist. No matter how sweet and innocent your leading characters, make awful things happen to them—in order that the reader may see what they are made of."

— Kurt Vonnegut

"Sweet" is not the first adjective anyone would choose to describe Aldo Zelnick (maybe the fourth or fifth, and only with much qualification), yet Vonnegut's writing advice still applies. While Aldo has had myriad character-testing misadventures already in this series, in *Mooch* he finds himself in real danger. After all, we figured, he is headed for middle school, and this book is number 13 in the series. Let's see what happens when we sadistically pair indoorsperson Aldo with a kid he doesn't know well and drop them into the backcountry together.

Awful things happened, that's what. But also marvelous things. And maybe a miniscule modicum of maturation. Plus we got to accompany Aldo to Great Sand Dunes National Park, Mesa Verde National Park, Four Corners, Manti-La Sal National Forest, Bears Ears National Monument, Moab, and even The Wild Animal Sanctuary. All of us who are fortunate to live within spitting (or driving) distance of these treasures know they're worth immortalizing.

We'd like to offer first our *mea culpas* for this book's delays (sometimes awful things happen in real life too) and second, our monumental gratitude. We're so lucky we get to create. We're so grateful this series still has a "hey-when's-the-next-book-coming-out?" following. And we're so fortunate we have marvelous helpers on our side, like designer Launie Parry, the Slow Sand Writers Society story mavens, and Aldo's magnanimous Angels, whom whenever we send up a flare make us feel like we're not alone in the wilderness after all.

When we do school visits and the kids notice the A-to-Z pattern of our books, they often gasp and murmur at the realization that an alphabetical series means 26 books (though the youngest guess anywhere from 20 to 30). We're now officially halfway there. We've reached the summit and will soon head down the other side. Here's to momentum and plenty more merriment.

ALDO'S MAGNANIMOUS ANGELS

Halo There! If you're an Aldo Zelnick fan, e-mail info@bailiwickpress.com and ask for details about becoming an Aldo's Angel. Angels receive special opportunities such as pre-publication discounts, free shipping, naming rights, and listing in the acknowledgments (especially fun for kids).

Barbara Anderson

Carol & Wes Baker

Butch & Sue Byram

Michael & Pam Dobrowski

Leigh Waller Fitschen

Chris Goold

Bennett, Calvin, Beckett & Camden Halvorson

Terry & Theresa Harrison

Richard & Peggy Hohm

Chris & Diane Hutchinson

Vicki & Bill Krug

Annette & Tom Lynch

Lisa & Kyle Miller

The Motz & Scripps Families (McCale, Alaina, Everett, Lucia, Caden, Ambria & Noah)

Kristin & Henry Mouton

Jackie O'Hara & Erin Rogers

Jackie Peterson and Emma, Dorie & Elissa

John Schiller & Suzanne Holm

Slow Sand Writers Society

Barb & Steve Spanjer

Dana Spanjer

Vince & Adrianne Tranchitella

ABOUT THE AUTHOR

Karla Oceanak has been a voracious reader her whole life and a writer and editor for more than twenty years. She has also ghostwritten numerous self-help books. Karla loves doing school visits and speaking to groups about children's literacy. She lives with her husband, Scott, their three boys, and a cat named Puck in a house strewn with Legos, ping-pong balls, Pokémon cards, video games, books, and dirty socks in Fort Collins, Colorado.

ABOUT THE ILLUSTRATOR

Kendra Spanjer divides her time between being "a writer who illustrates" and "an illustrator who writes." She decided to cultivate her artistic side after discovering that the best part of chemistry class was entertaining her peers (and her professor) with "The Daily Chem Book" comic. Since then, her diverse body of work has appeared in a number of group and solo art shows, book covers, marketing materials, fundraising events, and public places. When she invents spare time for herself to fill, Kendra enjoys skiing, cycling, exploring, discovering new music, watching trains go by, decorating cakes with her sister, making faces in the mirror, and playing with her dog, Puck.

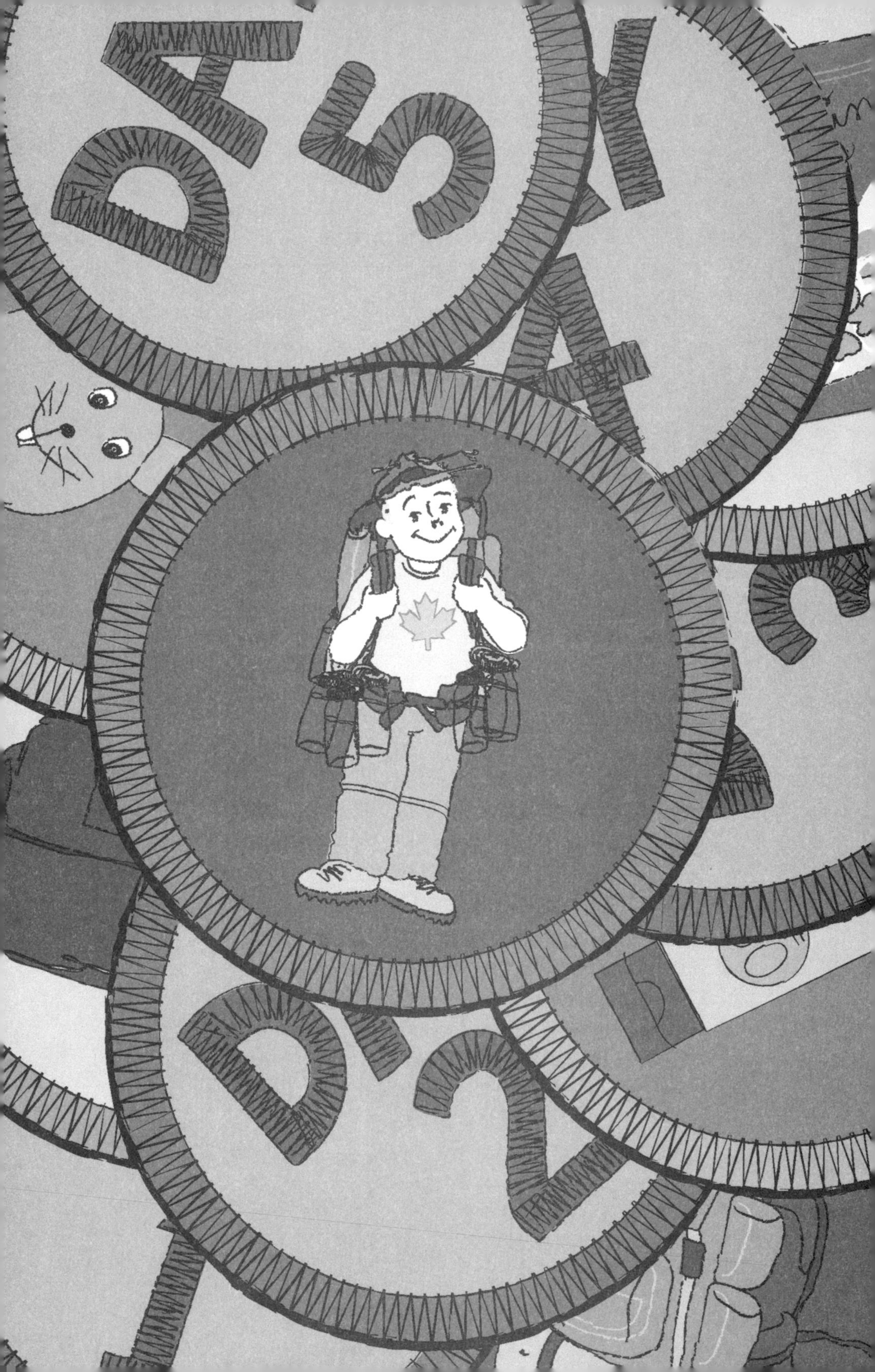